VEILED

A Novel by
KEN MCGEE

Copyright © 2023 Ken McGee

All rights reserved. This book or any portion thereof may not be reproduced or used in any manner whatsoever without the express written permission of the publisher except for the use of brief quotations in a book review.

For all my wild ancestors, who endured much
to allow me to write this book.

Much Madness is divinest Sense –
To a discerning Eye –
Much Sense – the starkest Madness –
'Tis the Majority
In this, as All, prevail –
Assent – and you are sane –
Demur – you're straightaway dangerous –
And handled with a Chain –

Emily Dickinson

FOREWARD

It was the worst of times. I suppose that seems a trite way to begin a book, but as a 32-year-old woman living through a pandemic, revolutionary changes in the social structure of her country, and a toxic election with its results disputed by a third of the country, it feels right. Although the great world created a well of sadness and strife, my small world of 2020 was just as bad. In February just after we all realized that the virus would become a true plague upon the land, I lost my job with Marriott hotels and parted ways with my boyfriend of two years.

Both of these losses surprised me because I had no idea that either relationship was in any way tenuous. Three weeks before COVID became a new word we all had to learn, my boss had discussed the vast amount of work that lay ahead in the coming months, all the conventions that were my responsibility. At least the company let me keep my health insurance through May. My boyfriend, who I always suspected liked me more than I liked him, disabused me of that notion just as I was ranting about not being able to go out on my birthday with the world shut down. He concluded that I was too negative for him during this stressful time, and broke up with me on the spot. I was so shocked that I left his picture as the background on my phone for weeks.

In the middle of these disasters, my mother offered to lend me a book or two and a jigsaw puzzle of an Edward Hopper painting (perfect). I could not be around my parents because of my father's high-risk status, and they stayed inside while I collected the large Macy's bag with my loot from their front steps. As I was leaving, my father cracked open the door and shouted that he had placed something special inside for me. Still in my car, I rooted around to find two boxes that each contained old papers fastened together with rubber bands. They had a bit of a smell to them and were written in two very different forms of cursive: one large and awkward, the other neat, flowery, and incredibly small. My father had added a note with them in his own precise engineer's handwriting.

Dearest Sarah,

I know this is a tough time for you, and it pains me deeply as a father not to be able to do more to help you. Although I stand ready to offer any financial support, I sense that this crisis requires something more than money to combat its effects.

Therefore, I bequeath to your care yet another diary written by your many times great uncle Fergal Dunne written in the year 1878. There is also a sort of account of the same period written by his possibly autistic daughter, Abigail. As you'll see, both manuscripts are barely legible and too confusing for my old brain to make much sense of.

Anyhoo, with some time on your hands I thought you might be interested in trying to decipher the thoughts of your long dead family members before these pages turn to dust especially since you did such a wonderful job on that Eads Bridge memoir.

Love always,
Your old Dad

It was all I could do to drive the fifteen minutes back to my condominium before starting in on the manuscripts, and I stayed up until three in the morning without getting two pages to make sense. My father understands me very well. I love mysteries, and I dearly love my old Irish ancestors. I put them in a book called *The Great Hope of the World* a few years ago. I assume that you have read it if you are reading this.

As my father mentioned in his note, the story in these documents takes place in 1878 in Saint Louis, Missouri. The city and the entire country at that time were in the midst of the Long Depression, which ruined many lives while creating impossible wealth for a few. Fergal and his sister Betha were doing well financially due to some smart investments on her part and a good job in city government for him. In addition to economic stress, America struggled with the status of freed slaves thirteen years after Appomattox. The Civil Rights Act had recently passed, but there was great uncertainty about what it meant and considerable reluctance to enforce it.

The status of Black people is quite personal for the Dunnes. Fergal's first wife Harriet was a freed slave and his daughter from that marriage, Abigail, is at the very least what was known as an octoroon, or one eighth black. "Octoroon" was one of many words in the vernacular at the time used to determine the status of citizens, and the question of whether someone could "pass" as white was very much on the minds of father and daughter.

The story that Abigail and Fergal tell takes place in 1878, as I said, which was also the first year of the Veiled Prophet Parade and Ball, that old Saint Louis tradition that continues, though with much less fanfare, to this day. Most people my age are unaware that the VP in the annual VP Fair held around the 4th of July in the city stood for "Veiled Prophet." According to my mother, when she was a girl, the Ball, replete with its coterie of society debutantes, was broadcast live on local television. She remembers the Prophet entering the Khorassan Ballroom to the *Triumphal March* from *Aida* and the young women appearing mostly bored with the possibility of being chosen the Queen of Love and Beauty.

What follows, then, is a story about Saint Louis told by long-dead relatives, but it is also about postbellum America generally, as it struggled with issues of race and the sudden creation of a new class of hyper-rich individuals (sound familiar?). Fergal and Abigail Dunne told their stories as well as they could while facing the socio-economic challenges they were born to face. Many of these conditions seem as terrible to us as ours will seem in 2163 if there are still people around to read about us. As a point of interest, all the great mansions in the tony Vandeventer Place neighborhood where the Dunnes lived have been razed and few pictures of the area even exist. The awe-inspiring gates that once surrounded those mansions sit next to the Jewel Box in Forest Park like the ruins in *Ozymandias*.

I have taken very few liberties with these stories. My editing has been mostly for clarity when the grammar or vocabulary of my dear relatives made their narratives incomprehensible to modern readers. Because Fergal's section was an actual daily diary, I did remove many of the entries of no real interest (the man was obsessed with what he ate and the quality of his bowel movements). There were also a few terms used by Fergal that have become too offensive for modern readers; I deleted them and believe he would have wanted it that way. Otherwise, this is their story, which I hope you are reading in a peaceful place. For the record, being a part of salvaging it changed my times from the worst to the best. I hope it does the same for you.

Sarah Dunne
December 2021

Chapter 1

FERGAL

It is with great trepidation that I set my pen to this blank page in the year of our Lord 1878, but I do so to attempt to rid myself of a melancholy cast of mind that has descended upon me of late.

Ha! What a bucket of crap it would be for an ignorant Mick like me to try to write in the manner of a gentleman. I can't, and I won't be doing it. Not only does it not come natural for me, the ink dries in the well if I try. The only reason I even know that word "trepidation" at all is from my association with a Mr. Max Niedringhaus, a truly learned gentleman who uses such words frequently and tells me afterwards what they mean. Why such a man is my friend, I am not certain, but I am happy that he is.

Anyway, that opening statement does have the truth in it, no matter the foppish way I wrote it. For some time, I have had moments where a dark veil seems to descend over the world rendering it not just without light, but completely void of any of the joy of life at all. I have tried to fix this problem in the way that men do; however, strong drink, though always helpful for a spell, appears to not be the cure for my situation.

I feel the need to explain myself. I am gainfully employed as a special assistant to the Mayor of Saint Louis, the Honorable Henry Overstolz, himself. It is not much of a title, but for a man like me who was born with nothing and received only a slight education, any title is a source of pride. The job pays me much more than a stone mason who breaks his back all day long and has additional benefits that are, in some ways, better than money. I live in a fine, foolishly big house in Vandeventer Place, the best neighborhood in the whole town, with great stone gates at one end and a fountain in the middle, as if built to represent the very streets of Heaven.

Of course, my residence in this lofty neighborhood is the result of living with my very wealthy sister Betha, a widow whose husband left her with a fine pot of gold. In many ways, I would prefer to live in my own place, but I am willing to tolerate my sister's many moods in return for free living. One would think that her being courted in the last year by wealthy man-about-town Stephen Peck would improve her mood, but Life seems to have hardened her as it does us all in the end.

I suppose I should come to the reasons for my particular unhappiness. During my short time of only 34 years, I have buried two wives, one in Tucson, Arizona, where I lived for a while, the other here in St. Louis just a few years ago. Harriet, my first wife, was taken by the typhus, leaving me with our daughter Abigail. Adeline Crain, the Saint Louis one, died from the childbed fever, the son she birthed following her a day later. Even as she lay dying, the poor woman apologized for leaving me with another child to care for, as if my suffering was the important thing. Anyway, that was the first time I remember the dark veil coming over me. Now it returns whenever it wants.

I should also mention that my poor daughter Abigail was born with some sort of brain sickness that strains the bounds of fatherly love. I hoped for many years that she might outgrow her problems, but, if anything, they have grown worse now that she is on the verge of womanhood. She suffers from many tics and starts of the mind which make her unfit for society generally. Worse still, her grandmother Martha also died last year leaving the poor thing with no one to care for her. I have hired a Madame Colet to fill that role as best she can and hopefully teach her to care for herself after I am in the ground. It might be working some, but Abigail's misery contributes much to my own.

Death calls to me now. There, I put that thought on the page, and the inky stain sits on the white paper asking to be crossed out, but I leave it alone. Those two wives of mine, women once so quick and alive, who are now nowhere at all, make me want to be done with Life. It might also be that the Angel of Death, if there is such a one, feels that I have cheated him all these years. The typhus could just as easily taken me or I could have perished in the great and terrible war that dragged so many, many young men below ground, a lot of them better men than me.

So it came to pass that some months ago I attended the funeral of our previous mayor Arthur B. Barret who served in the office a mere four days, barely managing to clean off his desk before succumbing to a fever. In the pew in front of me sat two Saint Louis swells, men stinking of money and property, having a conversation with no care as to who heard them. The younger one, it seemed, was suffering from the same sort of melancholy that I was, though his had to do with things he had witnessed at Vicksburg that haunted his days and nights. The man had been to physicians, men of the cloth, ladies of the evening, but none had cured his disease. When his older friend offered a solution, I leaned forward.

"My dear sir. None of that will assuage your troubled mind in the least. You must get control of these unmanly feelings before every swipe of the razor past your jugular as you shave yourself becomes a temptation." I was pretty certain that both of these gents were mostly shaved by barbers or butlers. Still, I strained to hear more. "You should start keeping a diary, sir, writing in it religiously every day, chronicling all the quotidian events as they happen. Only then, when you have transferred every dark thought onto the page, will they cease to have power over you, and you can return to your full vigor as a man."

About that time, the choir commenced to singing, and I heard nary another word from those two. I did not act on the advice at once as I thought it a queer idea, the sort that wealthy men might think of when pulling up their silk underdrawers while using words like "quotidian." I almost asked Niedringhaus about it, since he is the smartest person I know, but I felt too great a shame to admit a loss of courage to face up to the world. So I did nothing other than pour myself into work all day and pour whiskey down my gullet all night. Since that showed little sign of removing my veil of sadness, I have decided to try this diary business. I do shave myself most mornings, and a throat cuts so easily.

So here I am, about to spill all my secrets on to the white ghost of the page before me. Not all at once, mind you, because I may need to work up to it some. No need to rush.

Chapter 2

FERGAL

Not much happened this day. I did my normal rounds through the sixth ward with no great revelations at all. My work consists of talking to people of all stripes to determine which way the wind is blowing and see if the city government needs to set things straight. I am the eyes and ears of the Mayor (and sometime the fists and the boot) because here in America we have elections once in a while that are often lost by men who ignore the lives of the people who might vote for them. In all ways, this job is perfect for me, as I enjoy nothing more than talking to those who do things: the tailors, the carpenters, the dry-goods clerks. It is much better listening to their gripes than doing any of those productive things myself.

This evening I had an acceptable dinner of roast beef and potatoes. My mother-in-law Martha, who had been in charge of the cooking, passed away last year, and the meals have not been of the same quality since. Not that my sister Betha, sitting at the other end of the long table, cared a whit about the food. She merely nibbled at the edges of her plate as the corset pulls her waist into a tiny circumference (another word I heard from Niedringhaus) that only allows so much food in. She was in a foul mood because her suitor, Stephen Peck, was unable to dine with us due to something or other. I know that marrying the man will make her even richer, but I just wish she would find her smile. Maybe I should suggest that she start a diary. Ha!

Also at table was my daughter Abigail, straining to keep her nervous tics under control and eat like a lady. Madame Colet sat next to her whispering encouragement and directions. The French woman, who is as American as I am, always wears the simple, dark dress of a servant, yet somehow looks striking. I suppose I should mention that Abigail is an octoroon, which is one eighth African blood as near as I can figure. I married her mother out in Tucson where no one cared if she was a quadroon or a Red Indian or any damned thing. Under Missouri law, Abigail cannot marry a white man or do a lot of other things normal people do. Of course, with the right money put in the right place, the law looks the other way. I am more worried about her brain disease than her lack of a husband.

Young Ned, Betha's boy, was also there wolfing his food like an Irishman. He is a fine boy, but has not been taken to the woodshed enough for his own good. At least he has some fear in him that I just might drag him there myself, if he crosses me, which makes him keep a civil tongue in his head around me.

After dinner, I had a good cigar on the back porch and a wonderful trip to the privy. When I returned, I heard piano music coming from the parlor where Poor Abigail was trying to play the old song "Oh, Susanna" in a way I have never heard in all my days. The melody was mostly there, but it had a mad rhythm to it that made the song into something else altogether. Madame Colet, who has been trying to teach her to play, stood beside the girl with a great smile on her face. Maybe she should be happy as the other teachers I hired pronounced the girl hopeless. At least now, she was playing something, even with the queer sound to it. I gave her a nice bit of applause when she finished, and the poor girl bounced up and down on the bench with joy. I spoke gently to the two women so as not to stir Abigail into a fit.

"How about an Irish song for your dear Dad, then?" Madame Colet bowed her head ever so slightly at my request and rooted through the music on the table next to her. She showed a piece to Abigail who was still trying to calm herself.

"Oh, I know that one by heart, Madame!" After a moment of thinking, she began to play that new song, "I'll Take You Home Again, Kathleen" as her teacher sang the words in a fine voice with all the feeling the song deserves. Madame Colet is an Icarian brought to Saint Louis from France by way of Nauvoo, Illinois, when she was just a girl. Her people are well known for their musical talents, and I did not mind her French accent bumping against the Irishness of the song, not one bit.

After that, I retired to my room to attend to this writing business. There seems to be more to say about my situation, but I am suddenly quite sleepy. It appears that whiskey will not be required this evening, so maybe there is something to this exercise after all. Maybe.

Chapter 3

ABIGAIL

My name is Abigail Dunne, and I am the happiest person in Hell. My Aunt Betha, mistress of the great house where I live, uses that phrase betimes, but she actually says, "He'll be the happiest man in Hell!" applying it when speaking about a person doing a wicked thing that is nonetheless quite enjoyable, thus well worth punishment in the Afterlife. Most of my days I have felt as if I had sinned in some way without getting any enjoyment out of it at all, a girl living in Hell and none too happy about it. I will try telling you the story of how my life changed if I can manage it.

First of all, I was born an octoroon, which means that one of my grandparents had Negro blood. This makes me an outcast in Saint Louis where I live, not fit to associate with white people except as a maid or a wet nurse or perhaps a courtesan in New Orleans. (I tell you this at the beginning, Dear Reader, so that you can stop reading now if my situation offends you.) My Grandma Martha, the only one of my grandparents I have known, raised me since I was a girl. Although it is hard for me to believe that she was ever enslaved in that cruel system that existed until quite recently all across the country, it is the Truth.

My mother was also born a slave, but she was purchased and freed when still a child. She died of the typhus when I was still a child.

I suppose if this were my only defect it would be enough to cloud my days, but there is something even more wretched about me. I was born with a mental sickness that makes me subject to terrible fits. These are not the spasms of an epileptic that endure for only a minute or two, rather it is a condition of unease that is always with me making me unfit for polite society. I have an almost complete inability to be near other people for very long, even people I love, without being uncomfortable to the point of sickness or some outburst. From my earliest memory I cannot be touched for more than a few seconds or I will scream like the mad girl many say I am.

Wait. I apologize for such a poor beginning to my story. I thought it would be easy to tell, since I lived it, but it is not. I love to be alone and read feeling the way an author has such control over a tale with the revelations coming inch by inch in just the right way. I have just torn up a page after foolishly blurting out the ending, the secret of how I became so happy right at the beginning. It would be like Mr. Dickens telling you that the convict would become Pip's benefactor in the first Chapter of *Great Expectations*. (Sorry. I hope you have already read it.) I will try harder to tell this story properly. I should introduce some other important people.

My Grandma Martha will, sadly, not be in this story as she died a year before most of it happened. She always seemed to be the happiest person in the world, singing all day long as she toiled away in the kitchen peeling potatoes or mixing up the batter for Johnny cakes. Her death dropped me into a deep well of sadness where the water was dark and cold for a long while. I could barely get out of bed, eating nothing, waiting to follow her to the grave.

Some months after she died, when I thought my life was over,

Madame Colet, my new governess and tutor, arrived and saved me. She brought me many new books and showed me, without actually teaching, how to play the piano, a wonderful addition to my life. Our lessons consist of just talking about books I read and her answering any questions I might have as we walk in Forest Park. Most important, Madame does not see me as just a broken doll or some odious mess that has to be cleaned up. She is the first person in my life who accepted me with all of my tics and fits. Even my father and grandmother wanted me to be someone else; that is painful to write, but it is the Truth.

Let's see. Who else is important to this story? My father, Mr. Fergal Dunne, or "The Great Fergal Dunne" as he often calls himself, was born in Ireland and came to America thirty years ago with my aunt and my other long-dead grandparents. My father is very tall and stands always very straight when he walks. People call him "black Irish" because his wild hair is very dark and his eyes even darker, especially if something vexes him. Although he once sported a moustache, he is now clean-shaven though his bushy eyebrows are enough hair for one face. He has a very important job working for the Mayor of Saint Louis though I do not understand exactly what he does other than talk to people. Ever since his second wife Adeline Crain died in childbirth less than a year after they were married, he has changed considerably; at least everyone says so. I sometimes see him crying in the evenings, especially when he has gotten into the whisky. At such times I wish so much to be a good daughter to him, but I fail miserably. Although I try to hold my breath to keep from screaming when he places me on his lap or just embraces me too tightly, I cannot abide the contact long enough to be any comfort to him, and if I have some sort of fit, he feels worse.

My Aunt Betha, his sister, whose house we live in, was married to a Mr. Tidd, who must have been rich, as he left her a very wealthy widow. She is courted by another wealthy man, a Mr. Peck, who looks at me as if I were a mouse or some other pest to be exterminated. The house where we live is very big so I do not see my aunt all that often which is good because she always calls me "mad girl." I do encounter her young son Ned, my cousin, far too often as he delights in springing out at me from hiding places just to hear me shriek like a banshee. This seems to be fun for him. It is decidedly not for me.

I must also mention Mrs. Clara McPherson, our neighbor here in Vandeventer Place. She was once a close friend of Aunt Betha's though they seem to argue often about things that are very important to Mrs. McPherson, but not to my aunt. Once I heard Aunt Betha remark that if she never got to vote in any election, she would not give a tinker's damn (she can be coarse for a rich woman) causing Mrs. McPherson to leave without saying another word. I also do not care much about women's suffrage, but act as if I do because Mrs. McPherson allows me and Madame Colet to go riding on her land in Bellefontaine. I also remember that she was once courted by my father before he married Adeline Crain, but they seldom speak beyond the requirements of society.

I am nervous about writing about the next person, the most important one, because I find him almost impossible to describe in words. He is Mr. Max Niedringhaus, my father's friend, also an official in the Mayor's office, and the most perfect gentleman in all the world. He is polite, quite tall, sports a well-trimmed beard, and always has perfectly clean hands. None of that matters, of course, if he were not especially important to me. There is so much more to tell about him.

All of these people are important to this story, my story about how I became the happiest girl in Hell. I hope I can finish it. I am finding it hard to write about events as a person who does not know what is going to happen when I already do. You see, I know how foolish and wrong I was about many things, things I was ignorant of at the time.

This is much harder than I thought. I thought that it would be easier to control my wandering mind when I was alone, but writing is much harder than reading. Trying to put the world in order makes me want to scream and tear my hair out at the roots because the world, or at least my world, desires chaos. You will just have to stick with me until I get it right.

Chapter 4

FERGAL

It has been quite the busy day in Saint Louis. In addition to my usual rounds in the city during the day, I had a dinner meeting with the swells at Tony Faust's Oyster House and Saloon, the fanciest place in town and maybe in the whole damned country. I shaved for the second time this afternoon before putting on a freshly ironed shirt, my good suit, and my new bowler hat. It was a mild evening considering that July in Saint Louis can be miserable well past sundown. Regarding myself in the long mirror, I figured I was up for breaking bread with the rich folk.

It surprises me that we still have so many rich people in town, because times have been so tough since the Panic of 73. It hit the Eads Bridge Commission very hard, and some Chicago firm bought the bridge and the whole kit and caboodle out of bankruptcy. I was considering this when the girl answered my ring to take away my shaving bowl. She kept her eyes down and even did a little bow as she entered and left as if terrified to lose her position. Hard times for some.

I thought I might have a few minutes for a cigar before Niedringhaus arrived to accompany me, but he was already in the parlor talking to

Abigail when I came down the stairs. He has been stopping by more and more to visit her, which is a kind thing on the part of such an accomplished man. Madame Colet was there as well as a chaperone, I suppose, not that one is necessary as Abigail is still a child in her mind.

"Have you been waiting long? Why did no one tell me you were here?" I said this with a false anger that I immediately regretted because my daughter appeared ready to burst into tears, the poor thing. I tried to smile away her mood, but it was Niedringhaus who saved the day.

"It was my fault entirely, my friend. I came early to enjoy the society of some of the beautiful women who grace your fine home." Max had a way with everyone, politician that he was, but especially with the ladies. Although my daughter no longer seemed about to weep, her mouth flew open, and she might have run about the room had Madame Colet not tapped her gently on the back. The poor girl did not manage another word except to say, "Fare thee well" as we were leaving the house. It is a nice walk from my place to the streetcar stop up on Morgan, and I took the opportunity to ask Niedringhaus to explain the current economic situation to avoid any mention of Abigail.

"How can there be so many swells with bulging pockets around here when so many are one missed meal away from starving?" He smiled before answering. Smart men always liked being asked a question they can answer. I suppose all men do.

"Many of the formerly wealthy Saint Louisans have lost most of their money speculating in bad railroads and such. A large number of people that they once hired to do things are now unemployed and in very dire straits."

"I can see that, but it all happened so fast. I just can't see where the money went, and some seem to have more than they did before."

"Only the very smart or very lucky investors navigated successfully through this mess." He was referring to people like my dear sister who unloaded her Eads Bridge stock when it was worth something and then got rid of her silver before the bottom dropped out of that market as well. She took the advice of this Stephen McPherson, the New York financier who married her old friend Clara Hawkins a few years ago. He's a slick fellow, as are most of the Wall Street hooligans I've met. Niedringhaus went on about investments and capital, but I stopped listening. All my gold coins sit snug in an iron strongbox bolted to the floor beneath my bed. They aren't going anywhere unless I say so.

As luck would have it, young Bill Jones was driving the omnibus we boarded to take us downtown. I helped him get that job as a favor to his father who owns the best barbershop in town inside the Planter's hotel. Bill is a good worker and one of the fairest Negroes I have ever met. Once upon a time, there would have been no chance of him getting such a job, but with the war behind us, there is much good feeling in town for some things. He was in good spirits and seemed well in control of the horses and most of his corner of the world. He charged us no fare, of course, but I gave him some coins, as did Niedringhaus. Working men can't afford to be too fancy or they won't eat.

None of the working men I know would ever eat as we did this night. Tony Faust's up on Broadway and Elm Street was all lit up as we approached and packed with those who still had money to spend. The gas jets on top of the posts surrounding the place seemed to be blazing even higher this evening. From what I could tell, the rooftop terrace was already full, but the maitre'd told us our table was in a private section downstairs. While we waited to be seated, I snuck a peek into the ladies' restaurant to see who might be dining in that frilly place. I knew none of them by name, but enjoyed seeing the shocked looks on their faces at the appearance of my Irish mug.

George Bain gave me a warm handshake as he passed on his way out to smoke a cigar. He's the president of Atlantic Mills, the company that makes more flour than anywhere in the city, probably the whole country. He's also the Ninth Ward Alderman who wrote the Social Evils Act that legalized prostitution in the city for a few years. My old friend Cameron Claymore, now my boss I suppose, was already in the area shaking hands and slapping backs. As the Mayor's deputy, Niedringhaus and I reported to him alone. When he caught sight of us being led to a table, he came over, slapped our backs as well, and sat down.

"Boys, we have a spot of time before the Mayor and his pals get here, so let's dismiss the amenities and talk business."

"Can a man get a drink? I feel in serious danger of dying of thirst." Claymore motioned for a waiter, but went right into his speech as I ordered.

"This Veiled Prophet is going to be the biggest thing that ever happened in our fair city." I didn't look at Niedringhaus, but I knew what he was thinking. All these Saint Louis boosters, and Claymore was a great one, keep saying the newest thing would make the city the greatest place on earth. The Eads Bridge had been touted the same way, and as grand of an engineering miracle as it was, many men lost their shirts over it. Somehow, we still weren't the Paris of America, yet these men kept dreaming.

"But isn't that all for the society folk?" I wanted to say something before my drink arrived to show I was listening at all. Claymore waved his big hand.

"The ball will be for all the rich debutantes. You're right about that. But now there's to be a great parade, like the Mardi Gras down in New Orleans, only greater than that."

Just then, he stopped talking and rose to his feet as we all did, as His Honor, Mayor Overstolz, entered the room with a big group of well-dressed fellows. He nodded in our general direction before taking a seat at the big table in the center of the room. I recognized most of the men with him: two of the Chouteaus were there along with Erastus Wells and a bunch of bankers and lawyers looking fat and prosperous. The Slayback brothers, Lon and Charles, were seated on either side of the Mayor as if they were about to help him run the city, even though they haven't been here that long. Frank Addison, the Slayback's man, sat with us, the dignitary table being full.

I ordered the Beef Tongue Polonaise, which comes stewed in creamed potatoes. It is not on the menu, but Niedringhaus's friend Eugene Field, the writer for the *Morning Journal*, had me order it once, and I wanted it again. Niedringhaus had the quail on sauerkraut, which I will have to try some day as he assured me it was delicious. During dinner we discussed this Veiled Prophet thing some more. It seems the Slaybacks, who are originally from New Orleans, purchased $20,000 worth of Mardi Gras float decorations for $8,000. I assume they used the committee's money, but that was not discussed. It seems their man Addison will have much to do with the actual planning, so I wasn"t sure what was expected of me. I asked Claymore just that. Addison answered.

"You need to do whatever the Originals tell you to do." I did not like the man's tone or much about him at all. The "Originals" is what all these society men want to be called, those that are putting up money for this party. Sensing my displeasure, Claymore jumped in like the politician he is.

"We are all working together on this, my friends. If the parade is a success, it will show all those farmers in town for the Agricultural Fair what a great city we are." He clapped Addison and me on the shoulder at the same time to emphasize his point on our equality. "This could be the thing that puts us back ahead of Chicago once and for all." It turns out that he wants Niedringhaus and me to make sure the whole town knows that the parade is an important event, and we're to convince every citizen that disruptions will not be tolerated.

"This procession is not to be stopped by people or streetcars or anything else!" Addison sprayed food out as he said this. He has a nose that needs punching.

After dinner, Claymore asked me to go out and smoke a cigar with him, which meant he wanted to ask me for something without the others hearing. I was glad to leave Addison, but I missed talking to Tony Faust, who was about to come to our table. An amazing fellow, he never forgets a name once he's met you. Outside, Claymore didn't even light a cigar.

"I need you to attend to something for the Mayor." His voice was low, and I did light a cigar before nodding. I wanted him to notice that I didn't need any direction from Frank Addison or the damned Originals. "This Pulitzer fellow wants to buy the *Saint Louis Dispatch* at auction." He handed me a piece of paper. "You need to make sure none of the folks on this list bid if they know what's good for them." I tried to conceal my surprise. I thought the Mayor and Claymore hated young Joe Pulitzer, but politics change fast in Saint Louis.

"It shall be done." That was one of Claymore's things to say, and I knew he would enjoy having it said back to him. I looked at the names on the list. I knew all of them; none were dangerous, but you could never tell who they might employ to become dangerous. I asked when the auction was to take place.

"You have a few weeks at least." He looked about. "It should be enough time to explain the Mayor's wishes."

"It shall be done in any case." I repeated this with some joy that Claymore had confidence in me. Rereading what I just wrote I wonder if my pride of being the Mayor's man is a good thing or a bad one. Time might tell. I make very good money, but that's not everything. Nobody wants to be the richest man in the graveyard.

Chapter 5

ABIGAIL

Are you there? If so, I am glad that you are still reading even though I fear that I am raving. So many things are difficult for me with my mind sickness, but still I try very hard not to disappoint anyone. When she was alive, my grandma often let me help her in the kitchen to make myself feel briefly useful. She was very kind to me since I usually had trouble understanding exactly what she wanted me to do. My father and my aunt were not too keen on my working alongside the servants, but Grandma Martha, who mostly asked for nothing, overruled their objections. The other women working in the kitchen seemed quite ready to believe that I did the work because I am an addled family member.

"Martha, can I make the biscuits?" I would say that, never calling her "Grandma" when anyone could hear. Our relationship needed to be secret to support the ruse that I am a white girl. It is all part of living in Hell.

"Yes, ma'am, you can. Mix them up the way I showed you and then leave them be."

I loved making biscuits even though I needed her to keep an eye on me in case my mind wandered. It is really just mixing water, flour, salt, and bacon fat in a bowl, but there is a way of kneading the dough with your fingers (not too much) and an amount of time to wait before putting them in the oven (not too long). I could never get it right without her help, and the biscuits would never have been properly flaky inside or crunchy on top. I love her for showing me though I will never make them again now that she is gone. I wish someone could stand over me and help me write because I seem to be saying things that may not make sense. My thoughts are racing. I need to talk about Madame.

What did Madame Colet think of me the first time she saw me? I have never asked, but I imagine that she wanted to immediately turn on her heel and leave our house forever rather than take me on. After my grandma's death, my fits and starts had become well beyond my control causing me to stay mostly in bed to avoid seeing anyone. I spent hours counting the leaves on the big oak outside my window. So diseased was my mind that even reading, my great source of comfort, was impossible.

After my father made a brief introduction, he left us alone in my room as if the burden of my addled mind was now this poor woman's problem, not his. For several minutes after he walked away, Madame Colet said not a word taking a long time to remove her hat, which was really a bonnet of some sort. She also took out the stays from her reddish brown hair allowing it to fall over her shoulders. I don't know exactly why, but this action calmed me considerably. When she finally spoke, it was in a woman's voice that I had not heard before, gentle, but confident.

"As your father said, I am to be your new teacher." She looked into my eyes as she said this, a thing that most people never did for long, as if my madness might fly from me to them. "I can teach you many things about this world, Abigail, but there is one thing that no one can teach you. Do you know what that is?"

"N-n-no, ma'am." I admit that I stuttered terribly in front of her the first time we met, as if the demons in me were announcing themselves. She acted as if she did not notice.

"I cannot teach you how to want to get out of this bed and face the thousand natural shocks that flesh is heir to. I cannot teach you how to face them and stare them down because you want to be alive." She touched my hand for just the right amount of time before it upset me. "You must do that on your own."

I admit that I did not immediately heed her words, and for many more days I remained in bed. I suppose I thought she was just another hired servant, one who had to evince some kindness to me as part of her employment. Others working in the big house were nice enough in my presence, but I sometimes saw the faces they made, their mad girl visages, when they thought no one was looking.

Eventually I came to feel Madame was something different, and it was all in her voice. It was a voice that said, "I want you to be better, but I will still love you if you can't." Yes, it was her voice that won me over.

Chapter 6

FERGAL

Not too much happened out of the ordinary today, or maybe it did. I made my usual Thursday stops chatting with the proprietors and clerks in the downtown stores. They were all as excited about the parade as I supposed they would be. Saint Louis businesses have a way of bragging about their standing that I have not seen anywhere else. Prufrock-Litton has a great sign on the side of their store announcing it to be the "Finest Block of Furniture in the USA." Not to be outdone, Mermod and Jaccard's up on Broadway says it is the "Grandest Jewelry Establishment in the World." I haven't been in the all the world yet, but I question the truth of that statement. Anyway, all were quite pleased about the festivities and even the ball for the rich if it might mean they, themselves, could get a bit richer. That's America for you.

I stopped briefly in Hop Alley just off Market Street. I recognize that the Chinese who live there running laundries, tearooms, and lord knows what else, are heathens who can't vote in elections, but I do this and that for them just to have good relations. There are more ways to harm a city than voting wrong. Old man Shang, who runs the place with what appears to be an iron hand, assured me that his people would in no way impede the progress of the parade. As always, he asked me if I had an interest in the opium or one of the Sing-Song girls, but I only bowed to him before I went on my way.

As I cut across Lucas, a Major Gentry stopped me to solicit my help. It seems General Sherman himself is angry at the whole city of Saint Louis because he believes his water bill is too high. The major had some paperwork with him that I spent some time pretending to look at as we sat on a bench near the market. I agreed to tend to the matter, but it was hard to be interested in a wealthy General living up in Lucas Heights in a house some rich citizens of Saint Louis bought for him complaining about his damned water bill. Also, the major said General Sherman would be out west during the time of the parade and had no interest in it in any case. I have the same interest in his water bill.

My next stop was the Kerry Patch neighborhood where the poor Irish still live. Once a week I spend a few hours in the back room of O'Toole's tavern up on Biddle to take some rest while the people come to me. It's mostly the same, sad story with all the pregnant girls whose husband's knocked their teeth out before leaving for parts West, all the gray, stooped widows staring eviction in the face, all the men willing to do anything, anything at all to feed their families. It has grown worse of late with this Depression, and my meager collection of coins and worthless advice are all I have for them. I sometimes have a job or two to offer, say digging ditches for the city, but not today. I am concerned about the Veiled Prophet with this lot because even O'Toole, who claims to be running a business, spat when I mentioned it. I will suggest that the parade route be steered away from here. The poor can be distracted by a spectacle sometimes; other times they don't care for it at all.

After listening to the usual complaints for an hour or so, I'd about had enough of the Patch for one day when I noticed a young woman standing at the door as I prepared to leave. Although she wore a big hat cocked to one side and carried a parasol, her dress was shabby and cheap, and the brown leather of her boots was cracked considerably. She hesitated before entering my room, but she did not seem afraid. After she came in, she closed the door behind her.

"Good afternoon, young lady. What would you ask of the Mayor's office, then?" I motioned for her to take a seat which she did keeping a tight grip on her parasol all the while.

"There are many things the Mayor's office could do for me, but I'll settle for one." Her name was Aoife Monahan and in less than a minute, I determined that she was not connected with any Monahan I needed to care about. She was a pretty young thing, but with no smile to her. "My brother is in the Hoosegow, and I need to get him out. He's just a boy."

It turns out that this Aoife was something of a fallen woman who worked at one of the many such establishments in town where girls peddle their charms. I don't judge such things; she was supporting her big family the only way she knew after her Mick father fell off a barge and drowned in the Mississippi. As things happen, some customer had roughed her up a bit causing her foolish little brother to seek out the man for revenge. All he got for his troubles was a lump on the head and, because the person was a man with some connections, a trip to the City Jail.

"Were you born here or back in Ireland, then?" I needed some time to think about whether I wanted to do anything at all for her. The girl had a heavy brogue, so it was a common question.

"Barely. My mother carried me in her belly all the way across the ocean until dropping me on a boat up from New Orleans, so they say."

"Better that you don't remember that crossing." There was a silence, and I suppose she could tell by my changing the subject that I wasn't going to help her. Her blue eyes narrowed, and I could see her wondering what it would take to get her way.

"There's another thing. My older brother is Phelim Monahan. He is soon to return from New Mexico where he's been in the Lincoln County Wars. If his baby brother is locked up, he will start asking questions, and he could cause trouble that nobody wants. A few prominent citizens might find themselves with holes in them."

The Lincoln County Wars are much in the newspaper this year with terrible stories about the cold-blooded killers raging through them, a New Yorker named Billy the Kid being the most notorious. I didn't much care about this Phelim causing trouble, as the Saint Louis police are many and fierce, but I might have some interest in such a man for other purposes. Bradley, the turnkey at the jail, owed me a favor, and releasing one dumb boy for some rough stuff wouldn't take much effort on his part. In a second I made a great flourish as I wrote down the little brother's name announcing that he would be home tomorrow. Aoife managed a small thank you, but waited for me to go on.

"Will your older brother, Phelim, be upset when he learns of your current means of supporting yourself?" She almost smiled, but it was more of a sad grin.

"He would be, but I am no longer employed there." She reached up and lightly fingered the brim of her hat. "It's a bit of a mess underneath here. When I refused him something he didn't pay for, the bastard sliced off my whole ear taking my employment with him." She seemed surprised speaking that sentence, as if it summed up all the rest of her little life.

"What was his name?"

"I'll speak it never again. He's nothing but trouble for the likes of me, and I want no more trouble." She might have been about to cry, but the girl seemed like the sort who was done with tears. After a moment, she placed her thin fingers on my arm. "I have no money to give you for your help, but I can pay you in other coin. It would be nothing to leave the hat on." I patted her hand.

"Tis not necessary, colleen." The look of surprise on her face was the only one that slipped out of her control that day.

"But if it would give you any pleasure at all..." To be honest, some part of me wanted to accept her payment on the little cot just behind us in the corner. I am far from a saint. It is harder to be good man than a rapscallion, especially when I had to spend some time convincing her that my refusal had nothing to do with her imperfections. Again, the politician changed the subject.

"The greater pleasure for me, as an employee of the Mayor's office, would be in seeing you start a new life for yourself. Tell me, do you know your way around a kitchen? Because we could use some help at the house if you are willing to work."

The poor girl was truly overwhelmed then, and she trembled when I wrote down the address and told her what time to come by for work. As I gave her the paper she kissed my hand as if I were a damned saint. Jobs are hard to come by in this Depression. I gave her a few coins to get some vittles for her family and told her that I would like to meet this Phelim when he blows into town,

"You're a lady killer, Dunne, you are." O'Toole winked at me as I came out with Aoife looking like she had given herself to me. I left him to his own foul interpretation. When I got home, I told the kitchen staff that they had some new help coming, but I still need to mention something to Betha as she will be paying her salary. I don't think I will mention the girl's previous employment, though.

Chapter 7

ABIGAIL

Madam Colet shows me many things. I think I mentioned the piano and all the questions she answers. Once, she answered many I had not thought to ask. We were in her room, which was odd because we usually had lessons in the parlor or outside if the weather was nice. Her room was almost empty with only a small bed and an old chifforobe covered with many scratches. The floor and walls are bare and have nary a rug nor picture to adorn them. The quilt on her bed was magnificent though, with dark green and indigo squares and one big red square in the center. We sat on her bed with a book between us that said "Anatomy" on the cover.

"Abigail, I need to tell you some things. They are important things that most women are ignorant of, and you do not wish to be ignorant, *oui?*" Madame came to America when she was only five years old from France with the Icarians, so she occasionally peppers her speech with French. She speaks several languages and has taught me some German at my request. I love that the German nouns are considered masculine or feminine, so I can think of a chair with a moustache or a door with a bonnet.

"I do not want to be ignorant of anything, Madame." That was something she said often, and now I will say it forever.

"Ah, my prize student." What followed for more than an hour was an explanation of the human body, with much emphasis on the parts of a woman. The book had many drawings that were very useful to the lesson, and, with her encouragement, the questions tumbled from my mouth. One of Madame's many talents is as a midwife, and she went into great detail about the almost magic organs that grow a child.

"But how exactly does a woman come to be with child in the first place, Madame?" She appeared quite prepared for the question, and explained it by turning back and forth from the picture of a man to that of a woman.

"You see? A man in this way always sets the spark. Not every time, but he is always necessary."

"I see now." My eyes were opened about so many things that day. I will admit that over the years my cousin has been known to run shamelessly around the house with nary a stitch on before or after his Saturday bath for all to see. Still, I was truly ignorant of the scientific purposes of all this anatomy. "So this is true of all men these facts?" That was a fair question I thought, but her answer surprised me.

"Yes, even the German men, *mon ange*." I was not sure until that moment that she or anyone else knew about my deep, undying love for Max Niedringhaus. I did sometimes say, *Ich liebe dich*, aloud as I brushed my hair in front of the mirror, but I did not think anyone heard. Madame must have seen my distress as she turned her statement back into a lesson. "All men, the world over, have the same parts working in exactly the same way."

I must say that the discussion, especially the reference to Mr. Niedringhaus halted any additional questions that day, but my lessons were not over. Only two days later Mrs. McPherson invited me to tea at her house. I was very excited to spend time with her because she is one of the most beautiful women in Saint Louis, if not the whole world. She is also one of the richest since her father died of scarlet fever and left her all his money. Madame Colet took me on the very short walk over there, but she did not stay. It was just the two of us for lunch.

Mrs. McPherson's house was built by a very famous architect from New York and has many beautiful objects and paintings from Europe where Mr. McPherson seems to spend much of his time. Even the antimacassars on the chairs were little works of art. Her maids were all German women in very starched black uniforms who all smelled of strong carbolic soap. Two of them with very stern faces that scared me brought us tea and some tiny cookies called biscuits, but I could not eat one, as I was so in awe of being alone with Mrs. McPherson. She smiled very sweetly at me as the tea was poured, and it was all I could do to keep from bawling in my stupid way.

"So there are some things that we need to discuss woman to woman." I felt so many things when she said those words. I was overjoyed that she would consider me someone that she could talk to at all, much less "woman to woman." On the other hand, I felt a sudden fear that I had done something wrong and was about to be scolded. It turned out that she only wanted to help me in my motherless (and grandmotherless) condition.

"Yes, ma'am." I jumped back a little as Mrs. McPherson leaned forward and took my hand. She was wearing an artistic dress, a creation from which white silk seemed to flow forth in waves like the gown of a fairy princess. Her fingers were strong from all the riding she did.

"I've heard that you have some interest in the lightening of your skin, or your aunt has some interest in it. Is that true?"

"Aunt Betha showed me the wafers that she takes, but I didn't take one. I think she wanted me to." I was still not certain that I had not done something wrong. My aunt's skin is the whitest I have ever seen. I would have taken one of the wafers, but it scares me too much to be around her for very long.

"I'm sure that she did. Your aunt is quite vain about her alabaster complexion and wants the world to look the same. It is strange, because the way she dresses, she shows only her face." Mrs. McPherson's throat and shoulders were bare. "Nevertheless, you have no need for her wafers. Do you know what is in them?"

"No, ma'am."

"Arsenic, which is a poison, my dear. So your aunt is poisoning herself for some strange idea of beauty."

"Poisoning?" I did shed a few tears at the thought of that. She squeezed my hand.

"Oh, it's quite a slow process. Betha will live for years, and she will probably stop taking the potion once she is safely married." She laughed and threw a whole cookie in her mouth the way my father did. "But the true reason that you don't want those wafers, poisonous or not, is because you and I are true American beauties who always turn toward the sunlight."

"I don't know…" I did start crying then. I suppose it was her calling me a beauty, even comparing me to herself. I am used to thinking of myself as ugly with my coarse features, and she was like an angel come down from heaven. She took my face in her hands to calm me while I tried to breathe slowly as Madame Colet had taught me. She spoke very gently.

"My dear mother was a young girl in Saint Louis when it was still very wild and the cattle ran regularly through the streets. She helped my father clear the land for their first house guiding the mules to pull out stumps. Her whole life was lived outside either riding or working in her garden, and she always let the sun do what it would."

"She was dark?"

"Like a walnut all summer, and you should be too." She released my face to eat another biscuit. "I don't understand why Americans still care what all these British idiots think about beauty, though I find it truly funny that your aunt, an Irish woman, would ever desire to be an 'English Rose.'"

With that settled, the rest of our conversation was something of a continuation of Madame Colet's lesson on the anatomy. She provided me with a great deal of information that I suppose only married women know about. Clara (she made me call her that by the end of the afternoon) was very kind to explain so much to me so thoroughly. I also learned two words that day: "amorist" and "pessary."

Chapter 8

FERGAL

I paid a visit this morning to Rabbi Sonnenschein at Shaare Emeth up on Locust Street. There are lately quite a few more Jews in Saint Louis after that big Chicago fire in 71 left so many of them homeless up there. He listened politely to my story about the Veiled Prophet, but seemed to be in a hurry for me to be on my way. No matter. The Jews don't seem to want any trouble and generally vote correctly. You would think Niedringhaus would deal with them seeing as how so many of them are from the German areas, and he handles the rest of that ward. He always asks me to talk to them for some reason.

Speaking of Max, I had lunch with him at Von der Ahe's tavern up on Grand Avenue this afternoon. He has been at the house quite frequently to spend time with Abigail, and I even heard them speaking in German the other night of all things! I have some concerns about this courting, if that's what it is, and said something to Madame Colet about it. She reassured me that all was well. I assume the man just takes pity on the poor addled girl, and I will think no more about it. The father of a near idiot who is also an octoroon can't worry about everything. I took the streetcar up to Von der Ahe's with a great desire for a bucket of the home brew they serve there. Also, they have these wonderful sausages they call "frankfurters" in their German way. Niedringhaus was waiting for me at the stop and we talked politics for a few blocks.

"Do you think this Veiled Prophet will be good for the City?" Niedringhaus would only ask me that when no one was in hearing distance.

"I don't think about that so much." I thought that sounded like a dumb Mick thing to say, especially to a member of the Hegelian Society, so I tried to think a little more before I went on. "It seems the wealthy are all for it, so we had best help them with having their fun." He nodded, and I was glad to get a nod from such a smart man.

"Yes, but the whole thing is starting to look like just a way for the leaders of the community to assert themselves." That sounded right.

"Against the Unions, I suppose." The big railroad strike of last year is still a sore spot to many of the businessmen in town.

"The Unions, yes. The City passed all the new laws about needing permits to be able to march in the streets, and they want to make the point that they own those streets." Even though there was no one around us, he leaned close to me. "They also want to send a message to the Negro population."

"The parade sends a message to them?" I was uncomfortable discussing the subject. Abigail's heritage was a secret, but not one that was easy to keep. A lot of the old Saint Louis families, the original Frenchies, had Creole great-grandmothers in their lines that they never talked about, but Abigail's blood was not that old. This way of speaking to me, as if I cared one way or the other, suggests that Niedringhaus is aware of the situation. Maybe I should be concerned about his intentions.

"If you have seen the proposed appearance of the Prophet, a white-hooded man carrying a shotgun, you must understand the implications for the Negro." I said nothing, and we closed the discussion.

Von der Ahe's tavern, which is called Gemutlichkeit or some German name I can't pronounce, is quite the fine establishment. The beer is very cold with a bittersweet tang that makes it perfect for sipping for hours. There are raw onions in a barrel near the bar that merge with the great aroma of cigars to make it a man's paradise. If that wasn't enough, there is music, mostly from the piano player in the corner, but also from the many fine voices of the patrons who sing along with much gusto. Niedringhaus sometimes joins in with his strong tenor which is no surprise as he is a member of the Liederkranz singing society down on Chouteau. I would join in if they would sing something in English.

"Good afternoon, gents. How are you?" Von der Ahe was at our table right after we got our first beers. He has such a thick accent that sometimes I have a hard time knowing what he is saying. "My young friend tells me that you have an interest in the Paseball." Niedringhaus immediately said "baseball" to correct him.

"Does he say that now?" I have an instinct about people about to ask for money, and I could feel it just then as the man leaned toward me.

Van der Ahe went into a long story, so long that our frankfurters arrived well before he was done talking. They had some of the sauerkraut next to them that was wonderful. It seems that Von der Ahe started noticing some months ago that his place would suddenly be empty at certain times of the day. When he looked into it, he found that a great crowd of potential patrons was gathering in a nearby vacant lot to watch some fellows play the baseball. He became quite excited in the telling, and I had to keep looking at Niedringhaus for help with his words. Eventually he came to the point.

"Ja, ja. So. I have decided to purchase this Browns team as they are called. The Saint Louis Browns. They aren't really a team anymore, so I can do the deal for maybe a few hundred dollars." He grabbed my arm just as I was about to take a bite of food. "Then we will sell the people beer while they watch. It will be a gold mine. I even have an idea about putting these frankfurters on a roll so people can eat them as they stand there watching the game."

"Hard to eat that way." I was going to say it's also hard to eat when some barrel-chested German keeps grabbing your arm, but I didn't out of respect for Max who was clearly impressed by this talk.

"I will be building seats there, nothing fancy-schmancy, just wooden things." He grabbed my arm again tightly. "I will call it Sportsman's Park."

It turned out that Von der Ahe would let me in on the deal for a mere $100, and he acted like he was doing it as a favor to Niedringhaus. I told them that I would think on it, but I had already made up my mind not to invest in the business. I like my gold coins sitting all snug in that strongbox secured with a heavy Climax padlock. That's the gold mine I like: where the gold stays mine. Besides, this baseball seems like a passing fad with no money in it at all. Of course, I could be wrong.

Chapter 9

ABIGAIL

This is my favorite part of the story. If you really like happy endings, you should stop reading with this one. I would also tell you to stop reading *Romeo and Juliet* after Act II when Mercutio is still alive, and everything is well. It's a whole different story.

Maximillian Friedrich Niedringhaus's boots are always clean. Even on days when it would seem impossible to escape the mud and filth of the Saint Louis streets, his boots shine as if never worn. I suppose I noticed this about him because the first time he came to visit my father, I was lying under the dining room table as I often do to escape the people who might yell at me for sitting around staring. I was, in fact, staring at those boots while he talked politics with my father. None of that interested me, but something in the conversation did.

"Did I notice you speaking to that Mrs. Koch and her very nubile daughter at the Mayor's shindig the other evening? She's a beauty, that one, and I believe you could be just the man to remove that smirk from her face." I heard my father light a cigar, something my aunt usually discouraged in the house.

"She is handsome, but such things are only temporal to me."

"Come again?" My father clearly did not know the meaning of "temporal." I was quite proud that I did.

"I want a woman with a fine mind, one whose soul shines for me. That is much more important than her pretty face and pleasing figure. She must be *mein ganzes Herz.*" I did not know what that meant at the time, but I guessed correctly.

"Abigail!" Madame Colet called my name for some reason or other. Normally, I would have responded immediately rolling out from under the table to learn about the history of France or whatever, but I stayed put. I even held my breath.

"She must have wandered outside, Madame." My father introduced her to Mr. Niedringhaus, and the two of them conversed in German for a while. The smell of my father's cigar was strong making me turn my head and cover my nose for fear of coughing. Eventually, Mr. Niedringhaus's shiny boots and my father's scuffed ones departed, and that is when I found Madame Colet and asked for German lessons.

For many weeks, I listened intently to whatever my father might say about his day, even perching on his lap one evening while he was having his "toddy" which was mostly whiskey. He adored having a loving daughter and hugged me tightly while kissing my forehead. I fought the desire to scream and run out of the house to ask him in the sweetest voice I could find to tell me about the men he worked with. After an eternity of describing every alderman, ward by ward, he finally got to Mr. Niedringhaus.

"You would like him. He reads so many books, it makes my head spin. He's a member of the Hegelian society, of all things for a young man to join."

"I would greatly enjoy meeting him." I tried to sound only mildly interested, but I think my father saw through that immediately as I hoped he would. He does not like me much because my queerness makes him uncomfortable. He does, however, love me enough to want to see me have some part of happiness in this world. On the other hand, maybe he secretly hoped to find some man who would take me off his hands, the way that Atlas was tricked into holding up the world.

"I believe he would enjoy meeting you as well. You two can talk about books until the cows come home." I managed to smile sweetly digging my fingernails into my hand so as not to scream. Just a week or so later, he announced that Mr. Niedringhaus would be having breakfast with us. He said this to our new cook, the one who replaced my grandma, by way of requesting that she prepare a certain casserole for the occasion. I was reading about poor Becky Sharp at the time, and made one of my queer noises that is somewhere between a squeak and a moan; fortunately no one noticed.

Oh, how I trembled with anticipation during those next 20 hours. I wanted to do many things at once, but was not sure what to do at all. I rubbed myself down twice with a linen body cloth and even used the suede flesh brush that I normally disdain. I even considered stealing one of Aunt Betha's arsenic pills to lighten my face, but mostly I just looked in the mirror to pity myself for being such a freak.

"*Mon ange*, what troubles you?" Madame Colet heard me berating myself and lay next to me on my bed so that I could sense her presence without a touch that might make me hysterical. I told her everything, and she took charge in her way, calming me, making plans. The dear woman selected what I should wear (my azure walking dress with a "health corset" barely cinched to allow me to gasp some air). She twisted my hair into coronet braids which could easily be arranged in the morning. As she was finishing them, I looked in the mirror as tears flowed effortlessly from my eyes.

"Why am I so hideous?" Madame kissed me quickly on both cheeks catching a tear with each one. It was a sweet gesture but almost too much for me.

"*Mon canard.* This crying is not recommended for a girl who wishes to be appealing." She went back to my hair.

"I think that I am too ill to go to breakfast tomorrow." I touched my face even though a lady never touches her face. She gently pulled my hand away.

"I don't think so." She stood in front of me to look directly into my eyes the way she did when she wanted my attention. "You should go and meet this man, I think. But keep this in your mind every second that you are together: if he acts cold or less than friendly, it is only because he is afraid. Men are afraid of beautiful women and often act like asses to avoid having their pride damaged in any way. Think only of that."

I tried to fortify myself with those words as I descended the stairs the next morning as slowly as I could when my father announced Mr. Niedringhaus's arrival. On the way down I passed Aoife Monahan, the new girl, who was taking a tray to my aunt Betha. She ate only a hard-boiled egg every morning to keep her waist so perfect. I never saw her take more than four bites of food, even at Thanksgiving.

"You look very pretty today, Miss." The Monahan girl said just that as we were together on the landing. I thanked her profusely, but I almost started crying until Madame appeared behind me. At the bottom of the steps, talking with my father, was the man I assumed to be Mr. Niedringhaus, though I had never seen anything but his boots. He was much taller than I had hoped, and he had quite a nice thick head of hair, well parted and held down with only the slightest bit of pomade. My father, who was in good spirits, introduced us when I was on the second to last step. I smiled, but did not extend my hand for fear that he might take it and send me into a fit. Although I don't remember exactly what

I said, he paid me a lovely compliment that I also don't remember because it washed over me like a great wave obliterating any thought. I was somehow able to walk into the dining room on Madame's steadying arm.

"Will Mr. Addison be joining us for breakfast?" Mr. Niedringhaus said this to my father as he was pulling back my chair. I sat as gently as I could and even remembered to thank him. I must admit that I studied the young man furtively, yet completely, as he seated himself. His high white collar was heavily starched and only partially hid his lilac and white cravat. I breathed slowly to relax. Madame Colet did not eat with us, but sat in a chair at the edge of the parlor where I could see the back of her head and feel her presence for courage. I was very happy young Ned was in school; he was very successful at ruining my composure.

"No. He'll be arriving later, and we can go together to plan out this parade route or whatever it is." They discussed the impending celebration surrounding the arrival of the Veiled Prophet in Saint Louis while I sat and looked insipid. Mr. Niedringhaus wore a pale gray linen suit due to the terrible summer heat. A bright watch chain crossed his chest until it disappeared in his waistcoat pocket. His dark beard was what is called a Van Dyke, quite fashionable and extremely well attended to by his razor. Aoife served us breakfast quite efficiently, and the casserole was heavenly, what I could manage to eat. Once it arrived, my father was too occupied with it to continue conversing, and Mr. Niedringhaus actually turned and spoke directly to me.

"Your father tells me that you are a great reader. Have you read any of Mrs. Browning's' poems. I have not, but my sister enjoys them immensely." He almost tripped over his words, and I remembered what Madame said about men being nervous. I took a deep breath.

"I have not read her either." I could feel my cheeks burning, but I found some words. "Are you familiar with Mr. Whitman?" He looked at me in the way no man ever has, with interest.

"Yes, very familiar. There is a book called *Leaves of Grass* that I have read several times." He seemed quite proud of this feat. After a moment, he sat up very straight to recite in a deep voice. "*I sing the body electric. The armies of those I love engirth me, and I engirth them.*" He stopped, perhaps thinking that I found such an outburst foolish. Luckily, I thought it a game, which allowed me to respond in a voice I did not think I had.

"*They will not let me off till I go with them, respond to them, and discorrupt them, and charge them full with the charge of the soul.*" Mr. Niedringhaus's dark eyes expressed shock at my ability to quote Whitman, but also something else. He had a look of admiration, a look I had never seen before on any man. I went back to work controlling my breathing. My father, who had completely cleaned his plate, spoke up before we could continue.

"Well, I suppose that is poetry to some, even though it didn't seem to rhyme at all." He reached behind him and picked up a book from the sideboard slapping it none too gently on the table. "You should read this, my girl. It's by Thomas Moore, an Irishman, and it's all about this Veiled Prophet what's the talk of the whole town." I looked at the cover that read *Lalla Rookh an Oriental Romance.*

"It is really not so wonderful a book." As soon as he said that, Mr. Niedringhaus must have realized that he was contradicting my father. He quickly added another statement. "But it is quite interesting with the great celebration coming."

"Ah, the Irish never get the credit they deserve." My father punched Mr. Niedringhaus's shoulder in a playful way. "On the other hand, I could only get through three pages before falling dead asleep. It's all damned poetry."

We all laughed at that, and I found myself thinking that I understood exactly what was funny. I usually don't. That was the most surprising part of my first time meeting Mr. Niedringhaus. I mostly did not feel the slightest bit of madness in my normal way of wanting to throw my plate against the wall or scream hateful things or tear the braids out of my hair. I seldom do those things, but I usually think about doing them. Not that day.

"Ah, there's Addison." Frank Addison entered just as my father took out his pocket watch with some concern about the lateness of the hour. "You've missed breakfast, my boy." Mr. Addison was in a foul mood and waved his hand as he took a seat at the table.

"I am hardly your boy, Dunne, and anyway I have too much work for foolishness. We need to get this parade route figured out so I can report to the Slaybacks tonight at dinner." Addison was a short man with a long handlebar moustache. His clothes were quite rumpled as if he had slept in them. I had a feeling that he might have been staring at me impertinently, but I only had eyes for Mr. Niedringhaus. For Addison's part, he seemed more interested in Aoife Monahan, who was engaged in clearing the table. I do believe I saw him give her some sort of a pinch as she took away my plate. The poor girl dropped a fork on the floor which seemed to agitate her more than normal, and I thought that she might be about to cry.

"You should find a less clumsy one, Dunne. Some of the Germans work just as cheap and never drop a thing." Addison said this before Aoife was completely out of the room and well in earshot. I had a vague urge to throw the heavy vase in the center of the table at his head, but swallowed it as the gentlemen were set to leave. I followed them to the front door trying to breathe easily. Mr. Niedringhaus turned to me.

"It was a great joy to meet you, Miss Dunne. Perhaps we can discuss literature again soon. I get so few opportunities to speak to someone so well-read."

"I look forward to that, sir." I think I said that because Mr.

Niedringhaus took my hand upon finishing his speech. I heard my father say "oh" in anticipation of some fierce reaction from me, but there was none. For the first time in my life a surprise touch did not make me recoil or shriek. Instead, I actually held his strong, warm hand for the eternity of a few seconds feeling nothing but joy. When the door closed behind them, I whispered Mr. Niedringhaus's Christian name, Max, Max, Max, over and over as I stared at my hand.

Chapter 10

FERGAL

It is very late, but I need to write down my thoughts on this evening. I was just finishing a good dinner with some men who are trying to establish something called the Knights of Saint Patrick here in Saint Louis. The fellows were just starting in on me to convince the Mayor's office for support of any sort when I heard the fire bells. I could tell they were close, and I excused myself in short order as it's never a bad thing for the Mayor's man to be seen at a fire or any calamity to show that we care about the citizens. It was only a small blaze on the edge of Baden where the population is mostly German, but the mostly Mick firemen did a lovely job of containing it to two small houses. The houses were lost, to be sure, but better than the whole block. By the time I arrived, there was not much to do other than slap some backs and remind the crowd of the wonderful job Mayor Overstolz was doing.

Big John Byrne, captain of the brigade, took a pull of my flask and asked me to console a young mother whose son had succumbed to the flames. Usually, that is nothing for me to do as the words of comfort are always the same everywhere. I believe it helps a poor woman to hear them from a man in a position of authority who is better dressed than the ones she usually associates with. The speech was all there in my head as I walked to where she stood in the middle of a group of neighbors holding a toddler in her arms. I was all prepared to say how all was not lost since at least you have another son, one who needs his mother to be strong now to care for him. The right words were all lined up in my head and all ready to be shoved out of my mouth when I saw her face.

"I…" Not another word could I manage as I looked into her eyes. She had lost a thing too precious for words, and she only wanted me to help her get it back. All the commotion around her was merely a cruel reminder that the rest of us were doing our jobs and going on with life as if nothing had happened, when for her the world had turned into a desolate little orb. She hated this world just then and everything in it, herself most of all for continuing to live. I just stood there in front of her sobbing like a boy or maybe a madman. At one point, she actually touched my arm to console me.

Now I sit in my room making marks on a piece of paper trying to keep the dark veil from descending over everything. It is a sad truth that given the size of the world some poor soul suffers like that woman every second of the day. That is a terrible thing when you think about it. I wish I could stop thinking about it. I wish I could just stop.

Chapter 11

FERGAL

This diary writing, I must say, has had some good effects in combating my black moods. There could be some benefit of seeing your thoughts appear before you on a page rather than leaving the things inside your brain to rot there. Still, I have not written in two days as I am reluctant to see what I will say about recent events. Here goes.

Madame Camille Colet, who tutors and serves as a governess of sorts to my poor Abigail, came into my employment in an unusual manner. Actually, the woman did not come to me at all, but was thrust upon me by Sean Morkan, a good Irish Precinct Committeeman, who had helped me back in '76 on that city/county election (I'll confess that sin another time). Anyway, in '77 we had a great railroad strike, the biggest anyone had ever seen, that shut down everything. Nothing went in or out of the City for weeks. The Knights of Labor were behind it, and although I found many of their demands to be reasonable, the powers that be disagreed and put an end to the strike by the force of hired toughs and even the Army. Most of the leaders were arrested and thrown into prison. This Madame Colet had been a member of the Knights in some capacity, and although she was not imprisoned, she had been blacklisted by the wealthy from any teaching jobs in the city. The woman was penniless.

"Can't the Church do something for her? Kenrick talked big about the Union until the Mayor started busting heads."

"She is not Catholic, but she is a good person all the same. She felt a calling to help the poor working men in the way we politicians help each other." Morkan made his point. He knew I had some money and lived in a fine house; he was just calling in a favor for the business back in '76.

I thought for a minute about convincing that suffragette Clara McPherson to take her in since she likes women who can think for themselves, but she and I seldom speak now that she is married to a great financier. Going another way, I charmed Betha into taking her in as my mother-in-law's room was now vacant since she died. I told her the woman had a special gift that could help my troubled daughter and that I would pay for her keep. Even though I made the special gift part up on the spot, it has somewhat turned out to be true. Abigail has fewer fits than before and seems almost happy some days.

So I hired Madame Colet. The woman was, or still is, one of those Icarians who settled here in Cheltenham after they left Nauvoo, Illinois. (Hard to believe, but Nauvoo was once bigger than Chicago. Maybe not that shocking in crazy America, but I love to bring it up around these smug fellows from Chicago.) The Icarians, I understand, formed a community in which no one got to own anything, and they spent a lot of time on music and the theater. I can't imagine why that didn't work out, but there were lots of problems. Even Camille abandoned the group and married a Saint Louis fireman instead of moving to Iowa with what was left of the Icarians. After her husband died in the line of duty, she supported herself tutoring rich children until the strike business.

All was fine until two nights ago when I heard a tap on my door just as I started to open this diary to record the day's events. It was too late for Abigail, who sleeps like a rock once she gets there, so I figured it to be Betha needing some brotherly advice. I was surprised to see Madame Colet standing in the darkness of the hallway without so much as a candle to light her way. I held up my little kerosene desk lamp to make sure who it was.

She was wearing the plain black dress she always wore, but I noticed the milk glass buttons running straight up the front of it as they caught the light. Although I could not see her face clearly, I could smell jasmine wafting toward me. She must have spent some of her wages on fancy soap, a smart purchase I remember thinking. Her voice was but a whisper as she asked if she could come in and speak with me. Now the servants, and she could be considered one, come into my room day and night, and I think nothing of it. This was late, though, with the whole house snoring away, so I had a sense that I should send her packing. Instead, I stepped aside and showed her in, letting the jasmine fill my nose as she passed by.

Once in the room, she was all business calling me Mr. Dunne, but still whispering as she expressed concerns about my sister and Abigail. It seems that whenever Betha gets her Irish up, which is often enough, about some foolish thing my daughter says or any queer behavior, which is also often enough, she tells the girl that she will soon be sent off to the Insane Hospital on Arsenal Street. The Irish cruelty of it made me laugh some, but Madame did not find it funny at all.

"Your daughter struggles every day to be the person she thinks she should be. She has walked by that madhouse and is terrified of being locked away from everything she loves, especially her dear father." She paused. "I must say I understand her in that."

I am not given to succumb much to flattery as I find it unmanly, but she said that in her soft voice while we were alone with just the small light from my lamp playing across her face. Even though she is never trussed up in finery, Madame Colet is something of a beauty, a fact I convinced myself to ignore considering that she was in my employment. Alone with her and her auburn hair and light blue eyes, it was hard to do. She also has a strength in her, the power of these American pioneer women that overwhelms her lack of fashion.

"I will be speaking to my sister." I did not acknowledge her compliment, and a part of me, admittedly a very small part, wished she would take her leave. She did not.

'I worry about Abigail. She is so dear to me." She still spoke just above a whisper. "But I worry about you as well."

"There is no reason to be worrying about the likes of me." As I look back at it, I should have laughed at the idea of a servant thinking I would need anything from her at all. I could have put her in her place, the way a Mayor's man should have. But I let her go on.

"You have a great sadness in you. Abigail is a terrible burden for you as a father who wants her to be happy in the world. And I also know that losing your wife so suddenly set a huge stone of sorrow on your back that you have no idea how to remove. I understand. After I was widowed, I prayed for death every night for a long time because this world held nothing for me. I let my sadness live with me like another person, so I could grow sick enough of it to throw it out. You need to throw yours out and live some life." I tried one last time to set the woman straight, but her speech spoken from so deep in her heart affected me greatly.

"Madame, I appreciate your concern, but I must remind you of your position in this house. I am not the sort who takes advantage of a poor woman in my service." She gave me a smile I had not seen before from her.

"Yes, I know that about you. The other servants speak most respectfully of you, Mr. Dunne, saying they have no fear of bringing a cup of tea to your room or encountering you suddenly on the staircase with their arms full of laundry." She took a step closer to me. "For myself, I have no illusions about my place in this world compared to a man such as you." She sank to her knees before me. I thought she might have swooned, but her eyes were still clear as she looked up at me.

"Madame Colet, you must not. It is unseemly." I thought about pulling her to her feet, but I did not want to touch her. "I could never offer you…" I was trying to explain the situation to this crazy woman, but my words were starting to fail me.

"Marriage?" She laughed now like a brazen women in a tavern. "Don't be foolish sir. I feel something for you that has nothing to do with propriety or good sense. The Icarians were wrong about many things, but they understood that when society stands in the way of the pursuit of natural happiness, it is society that is wrong."

"Camille…" It was the first time I had addressed her by her Christian name, but I was not much of a Christian at that moment. I placed my hand on her cheek and she did not flinch one bit. "I am about to make love to you, unless you have some different idea about it." I knelt facing her.

"Yes, please." She said that in the way she might have said that she would like another helping of potatoes, with hunger, but no sign of sin to her. All the rest of that night nature was not impeded by anything except itself. She is quite the woman of the world, this Camille, with some ways of touching that were new to me and may be a part of the Icarian way. I'm not sure. She did lapse into the French some and kept saying "*J'aime ca*" which, even though I don't know exactly what that means, was like a hot spur in my backside.

So I have many concerns about this arrangement. I am not especially proud of it, but I don't seem to be wanting to do much to stop it, which might be what they put on my tombstone. It appears I want to live.

Chapter 12

ABIGAIL

It surprises me how difficult it is to tell my own story, but I'm afraid that my afflicted mind does not allow me to be clever about moving from one thing to another in a logical way. I apologize. One of the consequences of my malady is that I tend to think of everything at once, which is the same as having no thoughts at all. It is also the cause of my painful stutter that occurs when I try to say four things at the same time, the rush of words crushing my poor tongue. (I do not mention my stutter in this story all the time because it pains me so much.)

I shall return to Max Niedringhaus shortly, but suffice to say that he began to call on me or at least stop by the house for conversations about literature. Knowing much more now, I want to leave him for a while as his perfect self in that time when there was nothing but hope. I need to talk of other things.

One of my great joys that year was going to Bellefontaine to ride horses at the McPherson estate there. Clara (I started calling her that by April or so) keeps a large stable with five beautiful horses in it. She even gave me one of them, or at least let me name him, which is really the same thing. He is all black except for a little circle of white in the middle of his nose. For that reason I called him Silver Dollar, and he is as gentle as he is strong.

Before I go on, I want to say that I understand that many people would call me fortunate in that I have never known true hunger or the real horrors of poverty. Once, when my aunt and I were coming out of Barr's Dry Goods store, a gaunt woman with two thin children begged her for a few pennies to get some food. Aunt Betha pushed her aside. When I protested and began crying, she became angry and whispered to me that if I had been a poor girl back in Ireland, as she had been, I would have been left to starve to death rather than waste food on a mad girl. I must sadly admit that sometimes I see her point.

Still, I had Silver Dollar to ride all over the big estate. Clara and Madame Colet taught me to ride though they had very different ways. Madame rode sidesaddle mostly at a walk, rarely at a trot. Clara was seldom slower than a canter and loved to gallop, often going off the path and into the fields. In the little house there she always changed into her "cowgirl duds," which were men's pants with leather chaps and a denim shirt. On my third trip there she gave me a similar outfit and a western saddle of my own.

"Go on ahead, *mon chaton*. We can see you." Madame Colet often said something like that after Clara had run her sleek mare Farroe hard for a while, and we were all settled into a walk. They always seemed to have much to talk about as they rode which was fine by me. I loved feeling alone with just Silver Dollar as we made our way between rows of corn. I often talked to him about how I was feeling, and I swear he would shake his head as if he understood. I will also swear that after meeting Mr. Niedringhaus, I began to tell sweet Dollar about the possibility of romantic love, just like in Miss Austen, in my life.

After riding, I would stay in the stable to brush dear Silver Dollar until his coat glowed. Mr. Parker, who tended the property with his wife Hannah, fed and watered the horses and checked their hooves for any problems. Mrs. Parker was related distantly to the St. Cyr family. It must have been a great distance for her to have to work for Clara because the St. Cyrs are known for their great wealth. She was very nice to me, but I once heard her tell her husband in a whisper that she thought I had been touched "more than a little with the tar brush." That was the same day Clara and Madame were firing a pistol at an old scarecrow with much gusto. I wanted a turn, but they both said no.

Our carriage driver on these excursions was Mr. Nash, a very tall man who had once been a slave whom Clara's father had inherited and freed some twenty years earlier. Whenever we spent the night after a long day riding, he slept on a cot in the stable. Clara and Madame Colet slept in the second bedroom of the little house while I made a pallet on the floor. Those were the arrangements on the night after Max Niedringhaus, reacting to something I said, had taken my hand suddenly in his, holding it for several seconds.

I did fall right to sleep from the fatigue of riding so many hours in the sweet country air until a noise that was probably a coyote woke me in the middle of the night. Although I was somewhat frightened by the low howl, I went over to the window to see if something was suffering in some sort of trap. Sticking my head outside, I came face to face with a huge yellow moon perched just above the trees. I stared deep into its glow for a long time wondering whether Max might be seeing the same moon back in Saint Louis. I no longer heard the animal noise as the shriek of the crickets drowned out everything, even the prayers I murmured toward the moon.

I do not remember actually the doing of it, but I must have removed my nightclothes until I was naked as a newborn. In my head the moon was speaking the line from Whitman that goes "I will go to the bank by the wood and become undisguised and naked. I am mad for it to be in contact with me." I heard it as I opened the door and walked outside.

In the cool air I felt huge and small at the same time as my bare toes flexed in the dirt. I intended to visit Dollar for a conversation in the stable, but mostly I just reveled in the joy of drawing the ether into my lungs and pushing it out, as bats darted from tree to tree wanting to play some game. Coming around the big sycamore, I saw Mr. Nash, who I suppose had risen to take his toilet by the roots. He saw me as well.

"Nooo! What is the matter?" I don't know whether he recognized me in that dim light. He may have thought I was a spirit of some sort, but either way he was quite upset. His holler brought the whole household to us with even more shouting from Mrs. Parker who was the first to arrive. I heard her say the word "lunatic," and I stared right into her eyes before screaming as if I had just seen a ghost or was about to become one. Although I don't know if it was a true "barbaric yawp," it contained everything that was coursing through me that night, maybe my whole life.

"Enough!" Madame Colet said that as she threw a blanket around me, careful not to actually touch me. She did not scold me for the action though she did have some cross words with Mrs. Parker. It just occurred to me that all this happened before I had my anatomy talks with Clara and Madame. I think I am getting things out of order again. It's easy to do.

Chapter 13

FERGAL

The Monahan girl has worked out well in the kitchen; she has some talent at making biscuits, and Betha doesn't hate her. She wears a stiff maid's hat that covers both her ears, the real one and the missing. Better yet, her brother, Phelim arrived in town a week or so ago without killing anyone. Although he is not an especially big man, he has a dangerous air about him, and I could see the murder in his eyes. I hired him on the spot arranging to have him deputized so he can carry around his colt revolver with the ivory handle whenever I need him to. It turns out that this Addison fellow, the fellow who seems to be spoiling for a fight, is the one that disfigured the poor girl. I told her to say nothing to anyone, and I believe she will do that. In the meantime I will keep Phelim close just in case.

I don't know whether his reputation has preceded him or if his crazy eyes do the trick, but I have noticed that since he has been accompanying me on my rounds, the businessmen have new attitudes. After I admired a silk handkerchief at Barr's Emporium, Mr. Barr, himself, demanded that I take two of them on the house. The manager at Jacard's, that Beau Brummell Harold Green, gave me a tremendous deal on a new gold watch. I suppose it could be a coincidence, but my discussions with potential bidders on the newspaper Pulitzer wants to buy have also been most successful with Phelim behind me.

Camille and I now have signals, mostly at dinner, to indicate when a tryst is to occur. I continue to have much concern about this arrangement. I almost asked Niedringhaus about it, but he has often expressed his disdain for men who take liberties with their female employees. Even if I don't believe it to be that sort of thing, I suppose that's a common response made by most men after a good jagging, who don't want to own up to their sins. I imagine that Hegel fellow would be against it though I doubt he ever spent even one hot night with a woman like Camille Colet.

Chapter 14

ABIGAIL

Whenever Father had lunch at home, I became anxious on the off-chance that Mr. Niedringhaus might accompany him. One day I heard one of the cooks talking about a guest he was bringing home, and I noticed two of the other girls polishing the silver. Usually, the midday meal is of little consequence. My aunt Betha took her meals in her room where she spent most of her day, only emerging when she had transformed herself into the beauty she allowed the world to see.

I do not mean to chastise Aunt Betha for her vanity. I spent a considerable amount of time sprucing myself up for the possibility of a visit from Mr. Niedringhaus, even practicing my walk down the stairway five or six times. When Father arrived accompanied by a large Negro man in a dark blue suit, I was disappointed, but also intrigued. Although the house matron, Mrs. Barker, controlled her surprise at our guest as well as she could, I noticed that her breathing was quite irregular as she lead them to table.

I watched all of this from the top of the stairs where I was waiting to make an entrance that no one witnessed except Madame Colet who followed me down. Father introduced us to the man, whose name was

Robert Smalls, but who was actually very tall and had a great barrel chest and wide shoulders. Although I was not certain that I should curtsy to a Negro man, I did after I saw Madame Colet do so.

"Mr. Smalls hails from the great state of South Carolina and represents his district there as a Congressman of these United States." Father said these words slowly as if I were an idiot rather than just a mad girl who might not comprehend what an honor it was to have such a great man in our home.

"I was not informed we would be dining with two beautiful women, but it is a most blessed surprise." Congressman Smalls had a very deep voice, the sort that usually scares me, but the genuine kindness in it was soothing.

"You are too k-k-kind, sir." I did stutter a bit from the excitement of meeting such an important person, but Madame placed a finger on my back as she does to help me remain in control of myself. We had a very lovely lunch. Father and Mr. Smalls, while talking about political things, did not entirely ignore us. It seemed that the Congressman was in town to speak to Mayor Oberkfell, a meeting that had disappointed him.

"Your mayor is a good man, but I am afraid that he may be having difficulties with some attitudes towards Negroes that linger in a state that once allowed slavery." Father took a deep breath.

"Saint Louis, you must know, was one of the bastions of Union support during the War. General Sherman, a man known to many in South Carolina, lives not more than a mile from where we sit." Father is very passionate about Saint Louis being seen as a northern city, like Chicago. Mr. Smalls smiled.

"Mr. Dunne. One of the gunboats I piloted during the siege of Vicksburg was built at the Eads shipyard right here." He paused for a moment in honor of that battle. "The war is in the past now. What is needed, what President Grant did not understand, is that we must finish the great work begun by Mr. Lincoln. My people require only the opportunity to be a part of this great nation, but the time to fulfill the promise is now, before it is too late." Father nodded, but became more somber in his reply.

"The Mayor knows what is right, but he also needs to win elections to be able to do anything at all." The Congressman held up his large hand.

"I do not criticize, sir. My own state and, indeed, all the former states of the Confederacy, have begun to act as if the War had been decided differently. It fills me with great sadness."

"Yes, Grant got hornswoggled after the election of '76 with all the talk of fraud and made a bad deal. But it least we got to keep the Union and got President Hayes in the bargain." Father liked President Hayes, but Madame thinks he does too little.

"Yes, but it was a Hobson's choice, one that has left the Negro in the South virtually unprotected from persecution." He seemed more sorrowful than afraid, and that touched me deeply. It is not just because I have some Negro blood in me, but more the thought of people being cruel toward someone who has done nothing wrong. It makes me too sad for words.

"Saint Louis has none of that." Father was upset about any criticism of the City, but also worried about me having a spell. Although I was only shaking a bit, he knew what that might portend. I saw him catch Madame's eye, and she placed her hand on my back.

"And yet, we are dining here in your home because no restaurant in this town would allow us to eat together." Father seemed to forget about me.

"All of that will change very soon, I promise you. We have a large Negro population that has lived here as free men since well before the War. If, as you told the Mayor, there will be more coming from Mississippi and Louisiana because of the troubles down there, I assure you they will be treated well up here." The two men shook hands on that proclamation, and for a moment I felt that my spell would pass. Madame Colet removed her hand from my back to continue eating her lunch. The conversation turned to other things like the pot roast and the terrible heat. My father, of course, spent a considerable time explaining the Veiled Prophet celebration, and what a wonderful thing it was. At some point Mr. Smalls produced a copy of that day's *Globe Democrat,* setting in on the table in front of Father.

"Perhaps you could use your influence to alter the appearance of your prophet." Father stared at the paper and became quite upset.

"This is only the damned *Globe's* idea. I assure you this will not be how the Prophet will look at all."

About that time, I managed to peek at what had Father so agitated. Just beneath the bold letters announcing "A Prophet is Coming" was a drawing. It depicted a hideous man all in a white robe, his eyes covered by a hood. In his hands he held two shotguns and had a club tucked into his black sash. The eyes of the creature were dark slits and the thing's mouth appeared stitched together like the monster in Mary Shelly's book, a monster free to torment and terrorize the weak.

"Noooo!" I could not control the scream that pressed against my lungs until it came out. Father quickly turned the paper over as if I were a dog that would forget something once it was no longer in view. Without thinking, Madame Colet took me in her arms to comfort me, which made me worse. She began speaking very gently to me in that voice she has as the two men left us quickly alone at the table. She spoke in French, which did calm me, and I began to think of her as not of this world, the world that could produce that creature and put it on the paper for all to see.

Chapter 15

FERGAL

The auction for the *Saint Louis Dispatch* was this afternoon. Phelim Monahan, who has been sleeping in the carriage house, went over our play in the sale while feasting on his sister's biscuits and gravy. He and I had already "discussed" with potential buyers how this newspaper was a bad investment for them, and we needed to remind any who showed up just how bad it could be. As we were walking to the streetcar, he asked me out of the blue if my daughter had Negro blood in her. There was no malice in the question, so I answered him without anger. What's the shame of it anyway? We fought a whole bloody war to settle the question.

"Tis true. My first wife was a quadroon or maybe less. We were joined out in Tucson where no one gave a damn who you married." Phelim nodded in agreement, as I supposed a man who'd lived some out West would.

"You would think after the war, that after thousands of men died for the Cause that nobody would give a damn, but they keep coming up with these laws with this big word in it to keep whites from marrying anybody not white."

"Miscegenation laws. Our own congressman in Missouri wants to change the whole damned Constitution to go that way."

"Would that put my friends who took Indian wives in any trouble?" The man seemed concerned, and I was wondering whether he had one such wife back in New Mexico.

"I don't know. You never know what they are going to make legal or illegal in America. You just have to watch and see."

We took the streetcar downtown, but had to walk some as one of the horses pulled up lame. Saint Louis had quite a stink to it this morning, most of it coming from one of the tanning factories. Even though it was a block away from our route, the stench from the offal or maybe the process made us pull handkerchiefs over our noses and proceed almost at a run. I much prefer walking by one of the breweries, especially the Lemp, with the odor of hops and yeast giving a coat to the tongue. We eventually made it to the Lindell Hotel next to the Courthouse. Monahan had never seen the place and was very impressed with such a tall building with 300 rooms, they say. Even in that grand location the air this morning was especially bad, the smoke so thick that you could barely see half a block. It takes some of the thrill out of living in the city, but all those factories belch out the money.

"Good morning, Gents. Jesus, I need to go back inside for some fresh air." Claymore was standing in front of the hotel to greet us. He was smoking a big cigar.

"Pulitzer here?" I said this in a low voice as there were quite a few people going by on Washington Avenue though most of them clutched handkerchiefs to their faces paying us no mind at all. Claymore leaned in and spoke even lower.

"Yes, but it's not the best idea to be seen with him to avoid suspicion of any skullduggery." I nodded, but was not thrilled that this Pulitzer has become such an important person all of a sudden. He is younger than me and buying his own newspaper. I remembered just a few years ago when Tony Faust fired him for being a terrible waiter.

"Just curious about Pulitzer. How did the little Prussian get all his money then?" I was taking a small chance being so forward with Claymore, but he didn't seem perturbed.

"Ah, that's interesting. He invested in Eads' project to dredge the Mississippi down in New Orleans. I think the payoff was ten to one. What a country!" That bothered me even more since I passed on that particular investment. After a minute Phelim and I walked across the street to the Courthouse as Claymore went in to tell Pulitzer that all was well. Coming up the steps, I heard an old man telling a young girl that the dome of the Courthouse was modeled after St. Peter's all the way over in Rome. I learn something every day in this town.

From the back of the auction room I made note of who was who. Houser, the *Globe Democrat* owner, looked nervous about the proceedings. He was talking to Gratz Brown, who had once been governor of Missouri, and they were not in much agreement. The Knapp brothers of the *Missouri Republican,* the newspaper I read when I read one, seemed excited about something. I made sure that they all noticed I was there watching everything.

"Good morning, gentlemen! I propose to sell for cash two newspapers – two live newspapers." The auctioneer was a wee Irishman named Murtaugh with a big voice, and I suspect he had a dram or two for courage before facing the crowd. I'd given it up before noon myself. With how well this writing is making me feel, I may forgo strong drink. Not entirely, of course.

The first paper on the block was the *Journal,* a rag of no consequence to me and apparently the bidders. It went for only six hundred dollars. With that business done Murtaugh made a great speech singing the praises of the *Evening Dispatch,* a newspaper that "will live when all the other evening papers are dead." This drew much laughter from the crowd. In the corner of the room Pulitzer showed no emotion.

"I will open for one thousand dollars." Simon Arnold started things off as I knew he would. Arnold worked for Rosenblatt, the City Collector, but was bidding for Pulitzer (at my direction). The Prussian didn't want anyone to think that he thought the paper especially valuable. Someone raised fifty (another of my plants), and after a pause Rosenblatt went to twelve hundred dollars. Impressed, Murtaugh pointed his finger around the room, pausing to discharge some tobacco juice deftly into a spittoon before picking up his gavel.

"Fifteen hundred dollars!" A fellow just over from me, a swarthy stranger in a frock coat that needed tailoring, made that bid causing a great stir in the room. The man was a stranger not just to me, but to folks generally. When Buchannan, the reporter for the *Globe*, asked him his name, he only replied, "I'll tell you after a while." This was not a good thing by any measure.

The auction continued with Arnold and the stranger trading bids back and forth. Pulitzer gave Claymore a withering look as his man bid twenty nine hundred dollars. The stranger immediately went to three thousand. Murtaugh, who gets a cut from the sales price, had a great grin as he turned to Arnold daring him to reclaim his manhood, but the man shook his head. He was still shaking it when the gavel went down. I went immediately to the stranger and grabbed him by the back of his coat while the rest of the room was engaged in banter.

"Might I be asking you a few questions, my good man?" I flashed the shiny badge I carry from the Mayor's office quickly in front of his face. He let me lead him into a little coat room to one side. Monahan followed us in and shut the door behind him. No one saw us with all the backslapping going around. The fellow started to protest, but I shushed him.

"That man behind me is lately returned from Lincoln County where Billy the Kid was a personal friend of his. He would just as soon splatter your vile brains all over the wall as look at you." When the idiot reached into his pocket, he suddenly found himself with the business end of a Colt pistol stuck against his big nose. Monahan's hand was not as steady on the ivory handle as either of us would have liked, and for a moment I thought the man's head would be coming off at the end of a tremor.

"You can't just murder a man in the Courthouse." I thought that was a dumb thing to say on the off chance that the man holding the gun might be offended by it. I spoke very gently to keep everyone calm.

"You could be right about that, and maybe it would go poorly for us afterward, but you wouldn't be hearing a word about what happens tomorrow and tomorrow and tomorrow."

He smartened up quick, and we just stood there not saying anything at all until the time to claim the prize had clearly passed. I gave the poor man a ten dollar gold piece before shoving him out the secret door usually reserved for the judges' girlfriends. After spending so much time with a gun in his face, he was more than happy to part company with us.

When I returned to the main room, Buchannan told me that Arnold had been given another chance to bid on the paper when the stranger, who must have been a charlatan, never came forward with the money. I told him the fellow was just some drunk having a bit of fun with the City fathers. Arnold, or rather Pulitzer, got the paper for twenty five hundred dollars. I got a tip of the bowler hat from Claymore. I'll get my ten dollars back tomorrow, but I'll probably tell him it took twenty to get rid of the man after detaining him so roughly. All in a day's work to keep the city running.

Chapter 16

ABIGAIL

A wonderful gift that Madame Colet gave me during this time was the ability to play the piano. I have always had an interest in music, and there has always been a piano in our parlor though no one ever played it. My aunt's late husband, a Mr. Tidd, played it many years ago in Tucson, but since he died, it just sat in the corner with all the music stuffed inside it and no fingers to let it out.

The two piano teachers, who tried to teach me, were very angry and mean as teachers of anything seem to be. They showed me scales, wound up their metronomes, and then lost their minds with my inability to concentrate. I don't think either of them lasted more than two lessons before declaring me an impossible student. I suppose everyone, myself included, agreed with them, for nothing had been said about the instrument for years until Madame showed up.

"Just listen awhile to the sound and watch my fingers." She played the song "Dixie" by Daniel Decatur Emmet at a very slow pace by looking at the scribbles on the sheet music before her. I watched her play it twice. Sliding over on the bench, Madame placed my hands on the keys as they should be to start, and I pressed down a few times to get the feel of it. Five minutes later, I was playing it as well as she had, though she said it was superior because I was adding a rhythm that she called "syncopation" all on my own. I was so thrilled that I cried and kissed her dear hands. She tapped me lightly on the shoulder to show her affection without upsetting me.

"Show me another!" In my impatient, childish manner I asked for more songs wanting to dip my fingers in the music until it filled my head. I suppose I overdid it for the next week until my aunt limited me to only one hour per day. She was not always home, of course, so I was able to extend the time quite often. Nat sometimes danced around as I played, which was fine as long as he did not sing along.

Even though I'd been playing awhile before I met Mr. Niedringhaus, it took some time before I played for him. For the first several times he called on me, it was to bring me books he thought I might like. They were very prim things, which surprised me because he knew I had read Mr. Whitman, but I read them all the same, because, of course, I was in love with him.

I expressed none of my love as we sat in the parlor discussing Wilkie Collins or Margaret Oliphant while Madame Colet sat silently in the corner knitting. The piano sat in the other corner, also silent, until Mr. Niedringhaus went over to the instrument one evening to peruse the sheet music.

"Do you play, sir?" I was perched, as always, on the edge of my chair trying to look very ladylike. It helped that Madame always laced me tightly into a corset whenever Mr. Niedringhaus came to call. My posture was perfect, and the dull pain of whalebone against my ribs helped keep me from my sudden mad ramblings. My question, even to my ears, sounded like something Madame might say.

"I was encouraged to play as a boy, but I am afraid that my talents were quite meager compared to my sisters." I could tell that he could play and just needed some encouragement.

"Please play for us, sir. I am sure that you are very accomplished." He smiled, but did not play until he went on for a while about Ludwig van Beethoven, the great German composer, who was perhaps the greatest composer of all time according to him. Finally, he turned his back to me peering closely at the piece of music he had found. I rose and crossed the room to stand next to him, the corset giving me the courage of a knight's armor.

"This is called 'Für Elise.'" He sat very straight as he played staring only at the music, not noticing that I was just behind him. The melody of the song is haunting, but actually quite simple (he only played the first section) as the notes slide into one another, drift away, only to return and begin again. When he had finished, Madame and I applauded in a very unladylike fashion. He was quite proud of himself and turned to me.

"Do you also play, Miss Abigail?" He was the only person to refer to me in that manner, and I enjoyed having my proper name on his tongue. I was nervous, certainly, but something defeated my shyness. The tune that he had just played, which I could now see on the piano keys as if written there in India ink, had moved me, and I longed to feel it run up my fingers. He stood up and I sat down.

Without hesitation, I began playing the Beethoven for a moment as he had done, slowly with each note a precious thing. Then I changed the tempo to something that was not so much just in the mind anymore. I made the sweet melody jump right through my corseted hips to move the room around. I heard Madame laugh and clap her hands, and I also heard a sound from Mr. Niedringhaus that I hoped was not just one of shock. When I finished and turned around to look at him, he was shocked, but also elated.

"My dear Miss Dunne. That was an amazing performance." He looked down at my fingers that were still twitching. "How did you do that?"

"It just dawns on me." I was so happy that I almost kissed him right then and there, and I might have done something so stupid and impetuous if my aunt had not entered the parlor with her fiancé making everything prim and proper again.

So that was how our strange courtship was conducted. We discussed books and played at the piano with me altering every piece into something that was the same, but twisted around. I was so happy that I mostly forgot I was a mad girl.

Madame was the best of chaperones for our little trysts, not only helping me to make myself presentable, but also calming me with her looks when I became anxious. Often, she would excuse herself for a few minutes to get more yarn while we sat together at the piano bench. During one of these interludes, Mr. Niedringhaus reached over and gently squeezed my hand. The sudden touch upset me, but I was able to convince him that my reaction was that of an innocent maid who was delirious with passion. I think he liked that.

"You must not fear me, Abigail. I am a man of honor who holds you in the highest esteem."

"You are very kind, sir." I bit my lip hard to quench the fire within me. Even with my hysteria about being touched, I also longed for his big hands, the sharp knuckles barely contained by the skin, to grab ahold of me. I imagined that his touch might cure me like in some story where the blind can suddenly feast their eyes on the gorgeous world, but I was foolish then. I will stop now with myself frozen in that sweet innocence.

Chapter 17

FERGAL

This morning I met with the Reverend Samuel Johnson, one of the most influential men in the Negro community of Saint Louis. Seeing that his Baptist Church is up in the Eighth Ward, I took Phelim Monanhan with me as there have been some crimes in that area recently what with this Long Depression making so many desperate in need. Niedringhaus met us at Lucas Market because, even though I generally speak to the Negro citizens of importance, the barbers and landlords with most of the money, I thought the German, with his fine education could help in speaking to a man of the cloth.

Phelim waited outside the Church with one of my cigars for company, while Niedringhaus and I went in to speak to the Reverend. Johnson was in shirtsleeves rolled up to his elbows due to the heat of the day and was friendlier than any other man of God I have met as he greeted us both with a firm handshake. On the wall behind his desk were pictures of Lincoln, the young man without the beard, and Frederick Douglass with a gold cross between them with Jesus just above them. The rest of the walls of the small vestry were lined with many books with the overflow stacked on his desk. Even though that pile of books daunted me some, I decided to speak up anyway. I pointed to the pictures behind him.

"Isn't it grand that President Hayes made your man Douglass a Federal Marshall and in Washington DC no less?" I wanted to let him know that I was aware of the appointment and was even quite happy about it. He nodded.

"It was a great honor for Brother Douglass, and I pray for his success in that position." He took a breath and considered his next comment. "I also pray that someday in the near future many more will rise up, so many that no one will need remark on it."

"God be praised." Niedringhaus said that. I almost said "Amen," but was unsure of the Protestant lingo. Although Niedringhaus was raised Lutheran, I suppose he knows all the secret Prot sayings. It had a nice effect on the Reverend, and the two of them chatted back and forth for a while. I swear they talked about this Hegel fellow for what seemed to be an eternity until I could stand no more.

"We don't want to take up too much of your precious time, Reverend." Both men seemed surprised I was still in the room at all. "There's to be a grand parade through the streets of Saint Louis, and the Mayor wants it to be a great day for the City, so great the event could even become a yearly tradition." The Reverend switched his tone away from philosophy and on to business.

"Yes, news of this Veiled Prophet has reached us. Tell me, does it have anything to do with the Lord Jesus?" Niedringhaus seemed ready to jump in, but I didn't want them talking about any more damned books.

"No, it's from a little Irish story. Quite harmless and fun for everyone. There will be music and gorgeous floats for all in this great city to enjoy." I was trying to emphasize his inclusion in the festivities. He seemed uncertain.

"I'm afraid our Church would have very little to contribute to this parade as our finances have suffered much." I had heard that many in his Church had invested in the African Freedman's Bank which had recently failed. "These are very hard times, and, you see, the President has only appointed one of us to be a US Marshall to date." He was a clever man to act as if we might be asking for money to point out that he needed some. Niedringhaus pounced on the philosophical part of what he was saying.

"Reverend. So much has changed in so little time, but the best days are very near for all of us." Niedringhaus, as a member of the Hegelian Society, says things like that all the time, and he might even believe them. I couldn't tell what the Reverend was thinking, but philosophy hasn't bought anybody lunch yet at least to my understanding. You should always remember the best way to keep a man's loyalty is to keep money in his pockets. I spoke up.

"I failed to mention that we came here today to offer your Church a significant offering. The Mayor cannot be doing it himself for various reasons, but I can see that it happens to assist you in your great work of saving souls as well as promoting the peace." We understood each other, and I could almost see him preparing the sermon he would need to preach in his head. I wonder if there are any parades in the Bible he could refer to. I should read it some time. We all shook hands again with the matter settled to everyone's satisfaction.

Outside Monahan was not where we left him and nowhere to be seen with only a cigar butt left on the bench where he'd been sitting. We waited a minute, but Niedringhaus is not much for waiting on anyone. Borrowing the German's pencil, I left my card with a note on it to meet me back at Lucas Market and placed it beneath the butt.

Although I aimed to saunter slowly down the street to give Monahan time to catch up, Niedringhaus always walks as if he is going to a fire or maybe is on fire. I stopped on 11th Street to buy an apple from a little redheaded Irish girl who offered to do a little jig for an extra penny. I gave her two telling her to save one from what seemed to be her father watching us from the stoop in a drunken haze. After we crossed the street, I heard my name called out in a none too friendly manner.

"Dunne! Do you ever work or just gallivant around the streets all day?" It was Frank Addison, already in his cups, with two plug-ugly gents on either side of him. Both of their bushy beards looked as if they had never been touched by soap even once. I put the apple in my pocket and attempted to be a politician.

"Mr. Addison. How nice to meet you and your associates on such a fine day. We were just making certain that your little parade goes off without a hitch." His face went dark. It was obvious he was not happy with the word "little," but I didn't much care about his happiness.

"Posh! You haven't done one damned thing to help me with this project, Dunne." As he came closer, I could smell the whiskey on him. "I need you and your companion to head over to the Union Depot down on Jefferson and help these gentlemen tote some crates over to the warehouse where I can inspect the contents." I took a step back.

"You can hire all the strong backs you need at the depot for a dollar or two. Good luck to you." I tried to peaceably take my leave of the idiot, but he blocked my path.

"You know, Dunne, you remind me of another big Mick that used to work for me back in New Orleans cleaning privies. He didn't do that good of a job, but he did let us all have a good time with his daughter. Of course, I expect that was no great novelty for an Irish girl." He came very close to me. "Now get over there and start moving those crates."

I tried not to hit him, and with all of the political training at my disposal, I tipped my hat and stepped around the clod, only to have him roughly grab the sleeve of my good coat. For his trouble, he received my best punch in his breadbasket causing him to spew more of his foul breath in my face. I was hoping that his two henchmen would just stand there, but they seemed interested in a donnybrook. Niedringhaus bashed the bigger of the two quickly with the brass ball on top of his walking stick. After ducking a punch from the smaller one, he laid him out as well. The Irish like to fight, but these Germans just take their good old time and bust your head open.

"Sorry, boss. I needed to find an outhouse." Monahan, breathing hard from running, caught up with us as soon as the scuffle was done. There was something peculiar about him, but he was helpful, flashing his pistol around to encourage the two toughs to stay down. I pushed the wheezing Addison to the ground. A year ago I would have put the boot into all three, but I am trying to be more of a gentleman. I did give Addison a slight kick in the ribs to remind him to watch his mouth about the Irish.

Chapter 18

FERGAL

Madame Colet sometimes has Clara McPherson's boy, Jack, over to the house to spend time with Abigail. The idea, as I understand it, is to allow the girl to form a bond with someone she likes to shake some of the madness off her. I have no understanding of such things. Anyway, when I came home from my meeting at the Courthouse today, he was there on the parlor floor as Abigail played the piano. Little Jack was listening politely, even with some interest, but seemed a bit restless. As I watched him roll about the rug, it occurred to me that the boy I lost a few years ago would have been about his age if he had thrived.

On a whim I ran up the stairs into my spoiled nephew Ned's room. From a metal box on his nightstand, I fished out three of the fancy glass marbles that he hoards there. The things are all the rage now, especially since that German fellow invented the marble scissors that made them so cheap to manufacture. Back downstairs, I rolled one all the way from the foyer across the parlor floor to where it was stopped only by his little foot.

"Well, well. What have we here?" I said this in a low voice that only he might hear. When he finally realized what had struck him, the boy giggled. In a second he had grasped the marble and was holding up to his eye, entranced by the swirls of red and blue that ran through it.

"Mr. Dunne. I did not know you were home so early." Madame looked up from whatever she was reading to greet with a proper smile. When she noticed that Jack was holding something up to his face she asked him what he had. Abigail ceased playing and came over to the boy.

"Father. Jack is too young to play with marbles. He's only two and could swallow it." She went over to take it from him, but he pulled away placing the marble beneath his chest as he lay on top of it. I rolled another one toward him which he snatched quite neatly as it went by.

"I think the boy just wants some fun." I swooped down on him and held him up quite near the ceiling. It scared him for a second until he squealed with delight at being so high. He was a fine boy, sturdy and game for anything. I don't understand why his idiot mother dresses him in what they call a sailor suit. They are too frilly for a proper boy.

"Please, Father! You'll drop him!" Abigail was working herself into a fit, so I put him down. Then I made it worse by acting like I put a marble in my mouth and swallowed it. Little Jack thought I was the funniest thing he had ever seen.

"No, no. That would be a terrible thing to be doing." I pinched his chubby cheeks. "We can't have you dying on us before dinner." I picked him up again one final time before taking my leave. Abigail and Madame Colet picked up the marbles. I don't know why I am even writing about such a small interlude, but it affected me. I think I would have raised a fine boy if I could have had one. At least I would have been a better father than my own dad, though that would have a small hill to get over.

Chapter 19

ABIGAIL

I apologize again (and I probably will many more times) for being such a stupid young woman that I have let this story get away from me. I feel these things too much, I fear, which makes it hard to concentrate on the order things should be in. I wanted to mention something that happened some time ago while my grandma was still on this earth, but I forgot to say it at the time. There are many things similar to this incident, but I remember this one clearly just now.

It involved one of the girls who worked with the Hogans just on laundry day. I always thought she seemed friendly to me even though she also seemed angry most days as if she'd just received bad news. I was outside resting from the heat of the kitchen as the girl (I don't remember her name if I ever knew it) was returning to the house from hanging out the clothes to dry on the line out back. Under the cover of the bushes, I saw her stop to drink something that I assumed was spirits. I suppose it had the effect of loosening her tongue because she addressed me in a familiar way as she walked by.

"Playing at working, are you?"

One of the consequences of my disorder is that I cannot speak when someone seems angry with me, and the look on her face suggested I had done something wrong. I think she took my silence as a slight. Setting down the empty laundry basket, she lit a poorly rolled cigarette before blowing smoke in my face.

"You're kind of a dim one, ain't you? What's your name again?"

"Abig-g-g-g..." I was quite upset by then and my stutter made it worse. She mimicked it, but then laughed in an almost kind way. She patted my head like a baby as I was crying like one by then.

"Ah, don't be crying. It's all right." I wanted to tell her to leave me alone, but my jaw seemed locked shut. To my shame, I allowed her caress to calm me from a part of my distress. She was only taking a rest from tormenting me though. "Is that woman who cooks for the house really kin to you?"

"Y-y-y-y." I shook my head to indicate "yes," but I regretted it immediately when I saw the smirk on her face. Although I had been endlessly instructed to call my grandma "Martha" when others were around, I am certain that I failed to do that many times.

"Then that makes you just some little pickaninny living in this big house acting all white and grand when you are nothing of the sort." She peeled tobacco from her chapped upper lip. "Don't think about saying anything to your big Pa. I'll be leaving Saint Louis tomorrow to get rich in the gold fields in California."

"I w-w-w..."

"I just wanted to tell you I was on to you." She picked up her basket, but decided to say one more thing. "You should get hard, girl because the world is hard. They'll be throwing you into the streets soon, probably once your grandma passes. Can't be crying then." It took me several minutes to compose myself after she left, and I went right to bed. Grandma was concerned, but I told her nothing. I was too ashamed of my weakness to tell anyone.

I apologize for writing this.

Chapter 20

FERGAL

Niedringhaus and I were supposed to attend a gathering at the Cracker Castle on Choteau and St. Ange this evening. That's the great house that got its name because the fellow who built it made piles of money selling hard tack crackers to the Union Army during the Great War Between the States. Funny, how much money you can make from young men butchering each other. Still, it is quite a place arranged like a gingerbread cake with great, high towers all around. I was looking forward to seeing the inside of the place even if the party had still more to do with planning for this Veiled Prophet.

"So this cracker fellow lost all his money too?" I said that to Niedringhaus on the streetcar based on some gossip I'd heard from my barber.

"Yes. Pierce lost everything, including this house, through speculation in the wrong railway stocks."

"This damned Depression will get us all sooner or later. We might want to do some drinking tonight." I took a pull from my flask and Max had one as well. "I thought Claymore said Pierce was throwing this soirée."

"That's Pearce with an 'a' as in Charles Pearce, the lawyer. He bought the place when the other Pierce declared bankruptcy."

"Ah, me. The lawyers always come out on top in the end, don't they?"

All in all, we were both of a mood to get bollocksed. I suppose that was Claymore's thought when he got us invited, the free and plentiful booze to be a reward of sorts. He, himself, would not be attending, which was why I was surprised to find his fancy Rockaway carriage waiting outside the Castle as we approached the place. His driver, old Desmond McDonald, started waving a hand as soon as he caught sight of us.

"Gentlemen. I've been sent by Mr. Claymore, himself, to carry you to the riverfront where there is an urgent problem that requires your attention."

"What sort of problem then?" I was not happy with being so close to a good evening only to be fetched away. McDonald could tell, but puffed himself up with the prestige of having orders from our boss.

"That I cannot say, but it is of the utmost importance that I convey you two distinguished gentlemen post haste to the docks where Mr. Claymore awaits your arrival."

There wasn't much arguing with that statement though I came up near enough to smell Desmond's breath before I let him take me anywhere. He was only mildly intoxicated, so with heavy hearts we climbed into the carriage; we are the Mayor's men after all. McDonald put the whip into his mare whenever traffic allowed, and I needed a pull of the Irish to keep up my courage. When we made the turn onto South Market, I swear I thought we were going over. I was extremely glad when we finally stopped near the wharf without driving straight into the damned Mississippi, but I did not realize my troubles were just beginning. The steamboat *Belle Natchez* was docked at the first pier, and Claymore stood in front of it flanked by a brace of Saint Louis coppers.

"No time for amenities, boys. We've a great mess to clean up." He seemed a bit spooked for the man I know, the fellow with all the angles. "Have you handkerchiefs? Good. You should cover your face with them before going aboard." He tied his over his face like some outlaw, and we did the same.

I was not happy to be using my new Barr silk hankie in such a way, but I did notice that Claymore had only a cotton one, which made me feel slightly superior to him for once. We three masked men walked up the gangway to the boat leaving the police behind to stand guard. No sooner did Claymore open the door leading to the texas did I begin to hear the pitiful moans and sounds of helpless retching. One fellow, who might have been the captain, lay motionless in the corner with his fancy hat beside him. His skin was jaundiced, and his eyes, which were only open because he seemed too weak to close them, were of a similar hue.

"Yellow fever. The whole ship?" Niedringhaus said that while I was still overcome by the terrible sight.

"Almost all of them have some symptoms. They stopped in Memphis for repairs to the boiler, but they could have brought it all the way from New Orleans. There's no way to tell, but it's here now." We had all heard of the fever in New Orleans and especially in Memphis, but it seemed impossible to me that I was suddenly standing in the middle of it. I wanted to leave, but I couldn't. I was the Mayor's man and tried to think of something to say.

"Have you sent for a doctor, then?" The suffering of so many strong men laid so low touched my heart.

"No. And we won't be calling for one." Claymore was adamant about it. His eyes above the mask were hard. "This ship carries the remaining parade materials purchased from the Mardi Gras in its hold. If word gets out about this, the Veiled Prophet could be scrubbed altogether." I decided to pipe up before Niedringhaus and say what I knew he wanted to hear.

"I'll get some Micks that know how to keep their mouths shut and some big wagons to carry the lot of them down to the Quarantine Hospital." That's the new place down in Oakville for the poor smallpox and consumption patients that needed to be away from Saint Louis for a while. If it proves to be more than a while, they also have a fine cemetery next to the place.

"They should all have masks to move these people or to come aboard at all." Niedringhaus said that to me before turning to Claymore. "I will wake up my friend at Scruggs, Vandervoort and Barney to get some carbolic acid for us to wipe down the materials." He knew a thing or two about science and was not shy about showing it.

All the rest of the evening and deep into the night, we worked on the transfer of the passengers. I managed to find some dockworkers who weren't drunk and clicked just enough gold in their faces to get their interest. Although I gave them strict instructions to keep their yaps shut, I was pretty sure that no reporter, even one from the *Globe* would believe any stories their sort might be telling anyway.

By the time I returned with the men and three wagons and drivers, Niedringhaus already had his acid, and he commandeered two of the Micks to start washing the parade stuff before unloading it. To his credit, the German took off his jacket and pitched in to help the rest of us get the sick into the wagons. That meant, of course, that I was obliged to do the same. I had to carry some of the poor souls over my shoulder like sacks of flour hoping they wouldn't relieve themselves on me during the trip. I carried most of the women once I noticed the Micks taking rude liberties with the helpless things as they hefted them.

Claymore convinced the passengers with no real sickness at all to also ride down to the Quarantine Hospital just in case. The wealthy ones left in a separate fancy coach that he hired; the poor ones went with the sick and dying. Just one of them, a little dry goods salesman, disagreed with those accommodations, only to receive a small tap on the noggin from one of the coppers before we tossed him in. When we were all done, Niedringhaus convinced me to wash up using what was left of the carbolic acid mixed with some water.

"Dirty business, this political life, is it not?" Niedringhaus was tired. Instead of "this" he said "zis" the way the Germans do. "It surprises me the things they ask a man to do."

"It's a job." The diluted acid still stung my hands and arms, and I only rubbed a small bit on my face.

"Still, it surprises me the things they ask a man to do." He gave me a look to suggest that I might want to unburden myself of something, but I kept silent. What Niedringhaus could have been hinting at was a little thing that happened back in '76 and is the subject of considerable rumor.

We had an election that year to decide whether the city of Saint Louis and the County should part ways. There were powerful men on both sides who wanted the vote to go their way with a lot of money changing hands. The side Claymore, and I suppose Fergal Dunne, supported was the split, and that side lost. For a little while, it appeared the city and county would remain together forever.

Of course, there had been a bit of cheating here and there, but not so much as to notice. It took all my powers of persuasion, along with a visit from the best girl in Kate Clark's bawdy house, to convince a judge that a full recount of the votes was in order which he also put me in charge of. Now, my education was woefully poor, but I can count well enough. I also know how a bunch of dumb Micks *meant* to vote, even if they were too lazy to do it. So the City and the County have now gone their own way, and I doubt that it means too much one way or the other as no one with any sense will ever move out to the county. Those that do will soon be crying to come back; mark my words. On the other hand, I put a tidy sum in my strongbox. The whole state of Missouri can believe what it wants and go to Hell.

Chapter 21

FERGAL

This is the hardest entry I've made in a long time, confused as I am about what happened, but I suppose I just have to write it down. My sainted mother used to say that everything you get takes something away from you, the poor, sad woman. I am still trying, at the ripe old age of 34, to believe she was wrong, that there are some good things that have no impediments to them at all (Niedringhaus keeps improving my vocabulary).

To begin, I was invited to a party at the home of Mrs. Clara McPherson. She lives just across from us in Vandeventer Place in a truly large mansion built with money properly speculated by her New York husband. There is a great ballroom, too many bedrooms to count, and a horde of servants to keep it all clean. I had been there only one other time before this evening due to my feelings toward the lady of the house.

A few years ago, this Clara and I developed some romantic sentiments toward each other that blossomed into what we used to call "country matters." At the same time, my future wife Adeline Crain expressed a similar interest in me, enough to make my head swell with two women vying for my affection. However, before I had to make a choice between them, Adeline became in a family way forcing my hand to marry her and keep her an honest woman. At the same time Clara left town for New York City without even a fare thee well, only to return as the wife of this wealthy financier. When she moved into her Vandeventer Place mansion a few years later, she brought her new young son, though her husband seems to spend his time in London, Paris and everywhere else, but Saint Louis.

With all that water under the bridge, it did not seem like a good idea to partake of Clara's society at all. Since the woman and my sister Betha are still friends, she is betimes at the house for tea or some such thing, but I make myself scarce on those occasions. It is never a good thing to see your old loves after the fire has burned to ashes. That's always been my thinking, but since I started writing this diary, it has come to me that those fires always flicker, even from the grave.

Still, I found myself with an invitation to a dinner party at Clara's that had something to do with this singer, a Mrs. Williams, who seemed to be an important person to Abigail. She was also invited and desperately wanted to go. It appears that she has become quite friendly with Mrs. McPherson, who often takes her riding in Bellefontaine. I suppose I should pay more attention to her comings and goings, but I don't.

"Please, Father. I swear I will be as quiet as a mouse and not embarrass you in any way." Abigail didn't cry, but seemed about to or, worse, go into one of her fits. Madame Colet, who also knows Clara from accompanying Abigail to Bellefontaine, should have been the one to take her, but she was to be off visiting an ill relative, a Mrs. Jones in Chicago, making her unavailable for the task. When she joined in on the pleading, I found myself agreeing against my better judgement. Funny how women say they have no power, yet they usually get their way.

We went. I must admit that Abigail has learned something about getting gussied up to look like a proper lady, something I am attributing to Madame Colet's influence. Her hair was fixed up, and I could tell that she was using every ounce of self-control to keep from messing with it as she usually did. The poor thing looked terrified until Clara McPherson, herself, appeared wearing a robin's egg blue gown, what they call an artistic dress, and greeted us.

"Mr. Dunne. So nice of you to attend." I bowed, but did not take her hand. "Abigail! What a beauty you are! Will you please accompany me into the drawing room? There are some women who would love to meet you." She touched my daughter very gently on the shoulder as to not bring on one of her spells.

"My sister sends her regrets." I said that to be saying something as we stood there. I did not realize that I would be so struck by the woman's still considerable beauty.

"Yes. I believe her Mr. Peck is not much of an opera lover." There was a hint of sarcasm in her tone. I almost said that he and I probably agreed on just that one thing, but didn't.

After she steered Abigail to a room full of women chattering away, I snatched a flute of champagne from a tray that some servant was carrying around. I don't care for the stuff generally, but I felt the sudden need for a little Dutch courage. Pulitzer was there, but did not acknowledge me. Ever since he bought the *Post* and the *Dispatch*, the little Prussian now has two newspapers in town and must feel too grand for the likes of me. Eventually, I fell in with a group of three who ran the Olympic Theater, and one had a decent flask of whiskey he was sharing. I dumped my champagne into a vase and poured the strong drink into my fancy glass.

"This is quite a place, don't you think?" Rogers, the one with the flask, asked me that. I looked about some. There were some huge crystal chandeliers that impressed me, but also a dark painting on the wall right in front of us that did not.

"Could the painter not have put some smiles on this poor couple and used a little color?" It was all blacks and grays.

"It's called *L'Absinthe*. I think they are smiling on the inside." Rogers poured me another taste, good man that he is. "Her husband picked it up in France. The artist is some fellow making a name for himself." I looked at it again with even less joy.

"Where is the master of the house, then? Shouldn't he be greeting his guests around about now?"

"He's off in London or some place. We won't be seeing him this evening."

"If that Clara was my wife, I'd be leaving only after I put another baby inside her." This was said by one of the men whose name I didn't catch and received a great laugh from his associates. I laughed as well, but for some reason I had an urge to punch the joker's bushy beard up into his forehead. I was still considering it when we were called to table.

What a table it was, all glistening with polished silver that reflected the flames of so many candles. I heard some woman say "real lace" upon examining the tablecloth. The china plates were dark blue at the edges with two exotic birds perched on a white branch in the middle. There were little cards with our names written in calligraphy to tell us where to sit. I was surprised to find Abigail's name to the left of Clara. I was across from my daughter which gave me a good view of the hostess. There was a menu at every setting and some explanation of the evening.

I'm afraid I did not read the invitation very closely or else I would have known that this dinner was in honor of Marie Selika Williams the Negro opera singer, who was visiting Saint Louis. The woman, seated on the other side of Clara, was very young to be so famous. Although you might expect that she would be nervous in a room filled with rich white people, she and her husband, a burly man named Samson, seemed quite comfortable during the dinner. Marie had the look of someone who has lent money to everyone in the room and has yet to be paid a cent. Clara made a brief speech when we were all seated. I missed some of it because I was studying the menu.

"We are so honored to have Mrs. Williams in our home and in our city." I think she listed every opera the woman had ever sung. She did say one thing that bears remembering. "Marie Selika Williams will visit the White House later this year and perform for President Hayes and the First Lady, an occasion that I hope will mark the end of any form of racial segregation anywhere in our great land."

"Here, here!" I said that a bit louder than I meant to, not that I believe that the races will start mixing freely anytime soon (I spend a lot of time talking to people), but because I admired the woman's courage in speaking up for it. Although the applause that followed her speech was not robust, no one hissed or anything.

Clara gave me a smile for speaking up, and I believe she gave me several more throughout the meal. For my part, I will admit that it was hard to take my eyes off her. She has kept not only her beauty, but all her charm. She has this way of emphasizing her words, even in dinner conversation, with many great movements of her hands. Most fine ladies in Saint Louis keep their hands to their side. Not Clara.

After dinner, the men spent time in yet another parlor toward the back of the house where we smoked cigars and drank Madeira. Niedringhaus, delayed by city business of some sort, arrived about that time though I did not see much of him. At some point we were all ushered back to the main drawing room, a place big enough for dancing, where servants had arranged chairs for all. Mrs. Williams stood next to the grand piano where her husband sat unfolding a piece of music. As Samson played a brief introduction, she closed her eyes letting the notes sink in. When she opened them, they were the saddest I had ever seen, as if everyone she loved had died an hour before. She sang slowly and sweetly like a song in church, but all of a sudden she took a deep, deep breath and crushed the room with a sound that seemed impossible to come from one person. It was like a controlled scream, the kind that might be used to ward off evil or call evil into service. She did it twice in the course of the song; the second time a drop of spit flew from her mouth to land on my Irish nose. I didn't wipe it off until she was done. As everyone was applauding, I saw Clara look at me in a strange way.

About that time, I began to worry about Abigail who was not in the room anywhere I could see. When I did locate her, she seemed flushed and I suppose she had been in the back listening. Together we paid our respects to Mrs. Williams, and I noticed that Abigail's speech was beginning to repeat itself as it sometimes does. I decided to take the poor girl home before she had a fit. Our farewells to Clara were brief as she was still engaged in being a hostess; however, when she took my hand at the door, she placed something inside of it.

"That was the most wonderful night of my life. I love you so much for taking me. I will try to be the best daughter forever and ever…" Abigail went on and on like that during our walk home. I was a tad embarrassed because Niedringhaus decided to accompany us, but he did not seem bothered by her queerness. After he took his leave, I excused myself to take a much-needed trip to the privy leaving Abigail to prepare for bed, though she seemed too excited from the great evening to do much sleeping, I think. While there I looked at what Clara had given me. It was one of her calling cards with a short note on the back.

"Come to me tomorrow night at ten. Please."

I put the thing in my pocket and came up here to make this entry while the evening is still fresh in my mind. I am glad to have heard the great opera singer, and I am happy to have given my poor daughter such a memory (someone told me the name of that song was "Casta Diva"). This card disturbs me though as a married woman should not be giving out such notes to a man other than her husband. I will not be entangled in anything of that sort. The Mayor's man rises above such things.

Chapter 22

ABIGAIL

I am so happy to tell this part of the story about the wonderful night I had at Clara McPherson's, a night that was perfect in every way. The occasion was a party given to welcome the famous opera singer Marie Selika Williams who was visiting Saint Louis to see some relatives. I only wish that my grandmother could have been alive to see her, for Mrs. Williams, the renowned guest of honor, was a Negro woman.

My father took me there, but he seemed in a foul mood during the short stroll from our house to Clara's. I know that he once courted her before he married poor Miss Crain, and I suppose that seeing her as a married woman must have been awkward. Still, he seemed to recover his spirits when he got in with a group of men and the liquor began to flow. Clara kindly took charge of me as I think she could sense that I was nervous around so many strangers.

"Come sit with me, dear. Let your father talk politics and flirt with the women." I don't know if my father heard her say that, but he was quick to put me in her care. We sat in the small parlor that was filled with many beautiful ladies, well turned out in artistic dresses. One or two had the tiny waists and huge bustles of a different fashion, but they stood away from the rest shaking their heads. I didn't care if they were shaking their heads at me. Sitting next to Clara on the settee, I felt almost as if I were her daughter or at least a favorite niece. She was truly beautiful in a blue faille gown that someone said had come all the way from Paris. Her shoulders were mostly bare, and she wore a pink silk ribbon around her long neck.

All was well enough for a while until I noticed that I was wearing one blue and one black stocking. It was such a small thing that no one would have probably noticed, but it pained me to think that they might. (I had been so proud of myself for getting ready with no help from Madame who was in Chicago at the time.) I could feel a hysterical fit coming on the longer I berated myself for my stupidity. Clara, sensing that something was amiss, whispered to me.

"Come with me."

She arose from the settee, and I followed her, perhaps with a scowl on my face, because I saw one woman looking concerned as if I had taken ill. In a moment we were in her huge bedroom, a site that filled me with enough awe to almost forget my problem. There was a mirror that stretched from floor to ceiling in a gold frame. The room was large enough for a red velvet couch and matching footstool at the far end. The wood of the two chifferobes on either side of the fireplace matched that of the hearth itself. I could barely look at the bed, a big four-poster with a canopy edged in gold to make it seem like a crown.

"Do you need to rest, Abigail?" I gained control of my tongue enough to tell her about my foolishness. In a moment, she went to one of the chifferobes and returned with a pair of her own silk stockings. Sitting on the couch, I was too nervous to put them on, and Clara knelt in front of me to help. I started to protest, but she shushed me gently. Although I kissed her hand, I would have gladly kissed her scarlet slippers. When we reentered the parlor, I felt that I was the envy of all as those stockings made my legs seem to glow.

Before dinner I spoke to a Mr. and Mrs. Dorfman who knew Mr. Niedringhaus. She was quite friendly and charming, but he seemed irritated and kept checking his big gold watch every few minutes. When the subject touched on reading, I mentioned that Mr. Niedringhaus had recently leant me a copy of *The Phenomenology of Spirit*. Mr. Dorfman snorted.

"Imagine a female who can read Hegel! Most amusing." He seemed to think it was very amusing as he laughed quite heartily. Just then, there was an announcement by one of the servants that the guest of honor had arrived. Everyone began to move toward the front of the house. Clara whispered in my ear that she would take great pleasure in breaking Mr. Dorfman's nose.

Marie Selika Williams and her husband Samson, were holding court in the foyer when I first saw them. She wore a white gown with a very long train and carried a matching fan. Her hair was short and curly like my grandmother's. Although she and her husband were clearly of Negro blood, neither seemed anxious in the least. Mrs. Williams made an elaborate bow to Clara who made an identical one to her. I tried to copy the gesture, and Mrs. Williams gave me a warm smile.

The dining room was set up with two large tables for the many guests. Candles were everywhere making the fine silver shine even brighter. Dinner was a very elaborate affair, but I was too excited to eat much as I sat just across from the honored guests. Although the couple did not speak much during the meal, they were very intelligent and polite whenever they did. Sitting next to them, my father talked much about Saint Louis as this was their first time in town. I liked one thing that he said.

"Saint Louis takes some getting used to because it is several cities in one. You have all these people who would never touch a drop of liquor in this great town of booze. It seems old South and North at the same time with a whole lot of the West thrown in for good measure." I noticed Clara staring at him as if he were some great orator or something.

"I apologize, Mrs. McPherson, but the Mayor required me to miss this wonderful dinner party." Mr. Niedringhaus arrived as I was still staring at my untouched Blancmange, the prettiest piece of food I had ever seen.

"Apology accepted, sir." Clara rose and introduced him to the guests of honor. "You are in luck. The beauty of this gathering has yet to truly begin. Mrs. Williams has kindly agreed to favor us with an aria that she will be performing for President Hayes later this year."

When Mr. Niedringhaus asked after my health, it took every ounce of control to not launch into a conversation as if we were in my parlor. I only gave the most insipid reply worthy of the lady I was desperately trying to be. He went on to greet my father and several of the other men he knew (even Mr. Dorfman). After dinner, all the men smoked cigars while all the women who had consumed any food at all tried not to look miserable from the steely grasp of their corsets. To my great joy, Mr. Niedringhaus eventually spoke only to me even though several men seemed anxious for his attention. We talked about this Hegel. I understood that when the great philosopher looked at a table, he also saw the wood it had once been as well as the ashes it would become, but I was unsure how this way of thinking did anyone much good. Niedringhaus expounded on the philosopher for several minutes, but he did not enlighten me, no matter how much his voice delighted me.

Eventually, the guests moved toward the larger parlor that held the piano. Niedringhaus, still making some point, did not wish to join a crowd just yet, and we continued our discussion in the dimly lit corridor. Then a great silence filled the big house followed by a slow tune that spilled out of the piano and rolled toward us. It began on the black keys, mostly, drifting effortlessly to the white ones. I could see one group of notes as a question, only tentatively answered by those that followed, waiting for a greater answer to come. When it did, tears immediately filled my eyes.

"Casta Diva." Those were the first words that Mrs. Williams sang in a melodic repetition of what the black keys had been saying. I had never heard any voice so perfect, so pure as if the air pushed from her breast had been kissed by an angel. I could tell that Mr. Niedringhaus had heard nothing like it either as his eyes closed immediately. I could not even think in my usual way how I might alter the notes into anything different, so beautiful was the sound. Then, even from as far away as we were, I heard Mrs. Williams take a great breath.

What happened next was a perfectly controlled high note that made the boards in the house creak under the strain of it. The note went quickly from my ears to my heart where it wrenched even more tears into my eyes. It seemed impossible that anyone could ever hold so much air inside, so long did the great cry endure. When Mr. Niedringhaus opened his eyes, a single tear fell out seeming to slide down his cheek at the exact tempo of the music.

"Beautiful." He said at least that before I had my first kiss. I had thought about it for some time mostly doubting that I would ever be involved in such a sacred and terrible act. My face is too plain, my lips too large for anyone to ever want to kiss me, but Max did (I think of him as Max now, so I will refer to him as such). He sampled my lips considerably during the remaining moments of the song, and we were one entity until the applause in the parlor shocked us back to propriety.

"Love." I managed to say as he was wiping his face with a handkerchief. He may have thought that I was referring only to him, but I was saying what filled my mind about all the world at that moment. It filled me for the rest of the evening as I thanked Mrs. Williams and Clara in my best manners, as I took my leave of the people I will never see again. When Max walked back to the house with Father and me, I held both of their arms like a grand lady.

"You did well, daughter." My father tapped my back lightly after Max had taken his polite leave of us, and we were alone inside. Without thinking, I hugged him tightly, as a good daughter should, as he always wanted. For a moment, I believed that I was cured of my malady, but sweet moments always give way to others.

Chapter 23

FERGAL

One of the problems with writing your thoughts in a damned diary every day, is that any high-minded statement you make can come back to easily bite you on the backside showing you, and anyone who might read it, what an idiot you are. I went to Clara this evening. I walked over there telling myself that her word "Please" in the note was an entreaty that no gentleman could ignore. As I sit here, I know that being a gentleman had nothing to do with seeing her.

Like a moth to a flame or an Irishman to free liquor, I knocked on her door tonight right at ten as the note requested. I still carried myself like the Mayor's man as if she needed assistance with a political situation, but I was a fool. Instead of the servant I was expecting to greet me, probably that round-faced German maid, the woman of the house answered the door. She wore another artistic dress, a dark green thing, tied with a simple white sash.

"I am so happy that you accepted my invitation. I thought you would not." She held a small oil lamp that illuminated not much beyond her face (I saw the gown later), and the rest of the house was mostly dark behind her.

"Servants night off?" She laughed heartily, an unusual thing for a rich woman to do. Since my sister got used to having money, she hardly laughs at all.

"They are sleeping, of course, as are all people who work hard all day." She was not scolding me for my easy employment, just teasing. I had forgotten that she was good at that.

We went into yet another sitting room that had a few lamps lit in it. It was quite a feminine place with wallpaper that showed all these bright red flowers among dark green leaves. The heavy curtains that covered the big window had the same color of red in them with gold tassels hanging down. There were also lots of small figurines and vases on the fireplace mantel with a huge mirror above it. The chair she offered me was a pretty thing with a velvet seat, but was none too comfortable.

"Whiskey?" She had her fingers on a crystal decanter that sat on a little table beside two small glasses. I nodded, and Clara poured some into both glasses, handing me one before settling herself in the chair just next to mine. There was a silence that I thought I should break.

"I suppose we should toast to friendship." I swear I was straining to be a gentleman even as I held the very Devil in my hand. She smiled.

"It may be all we have left." She touched my glass with hers. She continued to smile, but there was a sadness in her.

"How can the Mayor's office be of any service to you, Mrs. McPherson?" The ward healer seemed the way to be just then. I also thought it a good idea to remind her that she was a married woman. She took a healthy swig of whiskey.

"The Mayor's Office cannot help in any great way, I'm afraid." Her face flushed as the spirits jarred her blood. "I'm sick to death of humanity, Fergal. All of the ignorance, and when you get beyond the ignorance, there is just cruelty and stupidity."

"There is an abundance of all of those to be found wherever you look." I took a drink then.

"It is truly disheartening to live in such a world." She tapped my arm lightly, but I felt it. "Last night was wonderful though. Mrs. Williams made me glad to be alive."

"She has a very fine voice." I was going to go on, but she held up her hand to stop me.

"Yes, but so many elegant St. Louisans, dear friends of mine, declined my invitation because they could not bear to break bread with a Negro woman, even one far more worthy than they will ever be." She leaned a little closer. "Your sister was one of them."

"Ah, well. It was probably her fiancé's doing. He has some family ties in Louisiana where people are less likely to accept the results of the War. I don't think Betha cares one way or the other about who sings the opera." I was not so sure about that. When Martha was still alive, she was quite adamant that no one know that she was my mother-in-law.

"Yes, I am aware of Mr. Peck's feelings, but a man changes a woman's thinking these days or else he wants nothing to do with her." A small clock on the mantel gave out a weak chime of the half hour. "Every woman should get to have her own thoughts, no matter what they are."

"Yes, I suppose they should." I figured that my reply would get a smile, but not the look I received from Clara, a look somewhere between a mother's love and a hungry woman watching as the stew is placed before her.

"I have missed you, Fergal. You have very few rigid notions about how the world should be." She threw back the rest of her drink.

"I had a poor upbringing." I left my drink alone and went back to politics. "Everything will be changing soon enough. We've the Civil Rights Act since 75, and that should give the Negroes all the rights they need."

"Yes, poor Charles Sumner died getting that through Congress for all the good it will do. The damned Supreme Court will overturn it soon enough in the same way they decided that women were too stupid to vote." She reminded me that she was still a suffragette, as if I had forgotten.

"At least we named a school after old Sumner."

"The Negro school." There was a long pause in which Clara was considering something. I thought it might be firing the Supreme Court, but it wasn't. "Do you no longer find me of interest, Fergal?" She appeared done with talking politics.

"I do, sure, but I am cautious about saying so to a married woman."

"I thought the Irish throw caution to the winds most days." She leaned close enough to me that I got the full effect of her scent. It was grand.

"We do quite frequently, but it often comes around to haunt us a little later." As we were speaking, she had begun to remove the fasteners that kept the hair piled on top of her head as if I were not in the room at all. I kept talking, my blood heating up. "These husbands can put a bullet in a man without having to explain much if they find him on top of his good lady wife." I thought she should hear such a crude expression considering that her status as a lady was in some jeopardy. She stood and placed a hand on her hip in a brazen way. I stood as well and backed away from her toward the door. I was still, even then, trying to think what the Mayor's man should do.

"You are well out of range this evening, sir." Her great mass of hair was now all about her shoulders.

"I thought it was fashionable for women such as yourself to have a great love somewhere in the world who you never touched or saw or did anything with other than exchange letters."

She laughed. "An unrequited love."

"If that is a word, and it means never getting more than six feet from someone, then yes." I was about that far away until she began moving slowly toward me, not seeming to take steps, but flowing forward like a mist.

"I'm surprised you read the English poets." She was close enough to reach for, but I kept my hands at my sides.

"I do not. My associate, Mr. Niedringhaus, tells me these things about Keats or whoever it is that you women swoon over in your female hysteria." Our noses were almost touching.

"I admire Keats." She gave me the slightest peck on the upper lip as she said the author's name. "I enjoy Shelley." She placed both hands on my chest. "But I adore Byron." Her eyes widened in that way they did when something pleased her. I breathed in her scent.

"You're going to Hell."

"Keep me company."

I kissed her then grabbing a great handful of her hair. One of the whiskey glasses was knocked to the floor, but did not break. I knew that her bedroom, the one she shared with her husband, was just beyond the doorway. I picked her up in my arms and carried her in that direction. Because she said something I did not understand, I paused at the entrance in case she had recovered her decency. She did not appear to, though she sensed my hesitation.

"I want more." That was enough to seal our fate for that evening. I spoke no more words of a gentleman the rest of the night, and, for her part, Clara said many scandalous things that would have been more at home in the mouth of one of the most round-heeled women in Kerry Patch. God love her.

I slunk out of there just as the servants were waking up. We did not make any great pronouncements of anything other than our affection, and I am certain the foolishness will not be repeated, as Clara is a mother who cannot afford to sink in the eyes of society. Although it is tolerated (even expected) for a man to have the Devil in him, a woman must appear chaste to all the world. Speaking of the Devil, I ran into dear Betha prowling around in her fancy dressing gown. She must have had one of her sleepless nights and only shook her head at me as I went by. She won't be causing any stir with me though. One of the men beholden to me in that business with the City/County election is Mr. Stephen Peck, who thinks he will become rich from it. Betha can't touch the Mayor's man.

Chapter 24

FERGAL

This is my first long entry in some time because I have been too busy to think, much less write. As if there was not enough going on between my trysts with Clara McPherson (fool that I am) and my late night visits from Madame Colet (perhaps bigger fool), I received an unusual request from Claymore yesterday morning to meet with the Knights of Labor. He and I were having breakfast down on Chestnut in the Laclede Hotel. I studied my eggs as I answered him.

"Not too certain how I'd go about that, boss. If I'm not mistaken, the whole lot of them were run out of town after the rail strike was broken last year."

"That's what the mayor and most of the others at City Hall believe, but I'm convinced that there still lurks some semblance of those thugs waiting to cause trouble for us."

"I think they would prefer 'hooligans' over 'thugs.' Sounds more Irish." I wanted to see if he was willing to laugh about the situation. He did at least smile which calmed me. Claymore mostly agreed that working men deserved better than what they were getting, but his current position required him to hold his tongue about it.

"Whatever you call them, I need you to find a way to make sure these union men understand that no disruption of the parade will be tolerated."

"It shall be done." I have no idea whether he knows about Madame Colet and her ties to the Knights of Labor, but he knows many things about what's going on in the City. One thing he didn't know until I told him was that Frank Addison has been skimming money from the Parade fund. A little skimming was to be expected, but it has come to my attention that it is more than a little. Claymore said he would look into it.

I have been somewhat besotted with Clara for several days and have paid little attention to Madame Colet, though she seems to suspect nothing. Luckily, Clara was to be at a meeting of the Women's Suffrage this evening. After dinner, I grasped Madame Colet's hand in a particular way that was our signal to meet. As if by magic, she entered my room just as the grandfather clock in the parlor chimed its twelfth time.

"I was wondering whether you had already tired of me." She had no frown on her face as she said that suggesting that she would not be angry if I had. She is a remarkable woman. I assured her that she still held my interest, more in deeds that any words I might have said. It may be my imagination, but I swear she could sense that she has a rival for my affection, and that spurred her passions considerably. Ah, these French women have some surprises in them. It took me a while to get my breath back to bring up the subject at hand.

"So do you believe that the Knights of Labor will ever be heard from again in these parts?" Although her head was on my chest and I could not see her face, I could feel her body tense.

"Why? Do you have some orders about them? Has someone approached you about me?" She was not frightened, as such, just preparing herself to hear bad news. I suspect that she has heard her share, the poor girl. I told her what Claymore had asked me to do. That seemed to relax her a bit.

"Can you get me a meeting with those that are left? I just need to make sure no one thinks disrupting the parade would be in their interest."

"Yes. It would take a few days to set up. And I would need to go with you." She touched me in a crude way, though maybe not crude for the French. "It could be an outing for us."

"An outing. Yes. We could do that."

"I will arrange it then, and we can make your little parade into something big." She touched me in an even cruder way.

"That would be grand." As a gentleman, I'll write no more about this evening.

Chapter 25

FERGAL

Saint Louis was hard at work as I looked out my window, all the smokestacks belching out the glorious filth of industry to turn the very heavens black as night though it was barely eight o'clock in the morning. It seems to get worse every year, which, I suppose, is the price for being a great city. Hard to believe there are yet so many poor people living here in the middle of all this. The Monahan girl, for instance, thanked me again for employing both her and her brother, as she served me my breakfast. She now sports a wooden rosary around her neck as one of the maids has been taking her to Mass. When I went to pat her on the shoulder, she kissed my hand.

I used some of the Mayor's money to hire a carriage to allow Madame Colet and me to travel to Cheltenham in style. The streetcar stops too far away from where she planned the meeting, and, anyway, I wanted my own rig waiting for me in case I needed to leave in a hurry. Camille (I call her that when we are alone, though she only uses my Christian name in certain moments) wore a bonnet along with her plain black servant's dress. She was so proper during the journey that the driver probably thought she was just a servant. I almost had Phelim Monahan accompany us as well seeing as how Cheltenham is mostly about heavy industry and has many rough men out of work just now, but I did not want to make the Knights think I was getting rough, not just yet. I instructed the driver to take us by way of Forest Park to see how that was progressing. Camille enjoyed the scenery and even stuck her head out of the window to draw some deep breaths.

"This is so beautiful. It's like a sudden trip to the country in the middle of all the soot that surrounds us."

"Vandeventer Place is as close to the wilderness as I ever want to be again. There are plenty of trees around to look at if you've a mind to." I was teasing her, but I truly don't share the views of men like Niedringhaus, who think there has to be a park on every corner, especially knowing how much they cost.

"Forest Park will be quite the gathering place once the streetcars can reach it. Families will be able to take lovely country walks with almost no expense." The woman is still an Icarian at heart.

"Yes, and there are even some plans to move the animals here from the Fairgrounds in the event that anyone needs to look at a bear or a monkey." She seemed impressed, but I don't see where all this money is coming from in the middle of this Depression. I really don't. Camille snickered at my disdain for Nature.

We exited the park and soon enough rode into Cheltenham. I am not too familiar with the place as we only incorporated it earlier this year. Now all these Micks will be able to vote, which will make them my business. Most of the good citizens, it seems, live in simple shacks, and there isn't even a Catholic Church for them to give money to, though the Bishop's man told me they are working on it. The one thing they do have is an overabundance of dogs; we saw twenty running loose on our short trip to the place we were looking for. Camille whispered the directions to me, and I called them out to the driver as if I knew where I was going.

"Ho!" The driver pulled up suddenly with some concern in his voice. I leaned forward to see three men blocking the little lane we had turned onto. At least one of them held a shotgun, and there was no one else around except the damned barking dogs. Camille whispered to have the driver stop where we were and wait, which I did. We got down out of the rig and walked toward the men, who wore black bandanas over their faces. I addressed them as confidently as I could while not looking at the shotgun.

"Good day to you fine gentlemen." The smell from the place, the mixture of sulphur and clay mining stung my nose. It may have been my imagination, but I thought Camille made a little sign with her hands like some secret incantation that calmed the men.

"You will follow us." The one who spoke had a hard accent like one of these Prussians that hasn't been in Saint Louis all that long. We went through a line of shacks and up a dirt alleyway that led to the back of a small building that claimed to be a tobacco factory by the sign on the side of it. The room we eventually entered with one man leading and two behind us was windowless and damp. My eyes had only started to adjust when the door slammed shut behind us so that I could no longer see Camille standing right next to me. I was just calculating how much these fellows would get from me in a robbery when a small oil lamp was turned up and someone spoke in a muffled voice.

"I am the Master Workman of the Knights of Labor. You are in the presence of the Venerable Sage and his court. Welcome to this sanctuary on behalf of the toiling millions of the earth." In the weak light I could see all the fellows were wearing long robes and hoods. The one seated wore a purple robe and must have been the grand panjandrum, the Sage fellow.

"By the sweat of thy brow shalt thou eat bread." Camille had told me to say those words as soon as I was able. She said them at the same time in a voice I had not heard before, a strong voice. The fellow in a red robe stepped forward.

"I don't know that you understand the meaning of those words, pally." He was directing this more to the Sage than to me. "You claim to be a friend to Labor, yet you work for the very man who broke our strike with violence and threw many of our leaders in jail." He chewed his words like a Scot about to lose his temper. I had only my cane for any scrapping, and I tightened my grip on it. There seemed to be a general agreement that I was a scoundrel.

"This man is a friend of mine, and I have done more for labor than the lot of you." Camille spoke up loud, as a man would addressing a crowd. "I was in the gutter after they broke the strike. He saved my life when none of you could." There was some whispered discussion, and I thought I should say something myself. It is not fitting to be defended by a woman. I cleared my throat and tried to not look as scared as I was.

"My friends. I do work for Mayor Oberkfell, that's the truth of it. In my job I am obliged to go all over the City, and what I see is all this wealth, all this power being raised up with none of it coming from nothing. No, it is all raised on the backs of working men struggling just to live another day." The Master Workman lifted his veil slightly and heaved a wad in the general direction of a spittoon. He missed.

"What would a rich man like yourself know about it?" I spat then myself making a satisfying little hollow ting inside the brass.

"Yes, I do reside in a fancy house just now. My family got lucky in this great poker game they run here in America, but I remember when I couldn't even get a seat at the table. I was just another poor Mick wondering if he'd starve or freeze to death." I let them think about that a minute. "And nothing will ever make the game fair until men in Saint Louis who live in big houses realize that the bricks that built them came from the hands of working men digging clay right here in

Cheltenham, that another group put on the roof, that everything in the house gets here by steamboats and trains run by laboring men. They need to understand that and also understand that all of those men are tired of living in such a rich place where they can barely put stew on the table some nights." There was a long silence until the Venerable Sage turned to Camille.

"Should we take this man at his word, sister?" She did not hesitate for a second.

"You should." She touched me gently on the sleeve of my coat. "He is a good man for us." They huddled briefly, but I think the Sage had made up his mind.

They all came forward then to shake my hand, even the Master Workman though he did his best to crush my fingers. They even showed the special secret handshake they have and agreed not to do anything to disrupt the parade. I pulled out my flask and we had a drink on it. Claymore has allotted me 20 jobs to work assembling the floats; I offered them ten, which made me even more popular. I was about to take my leave of them when Camille said that she wanted a minute to talk to an old Icarian friend who was just outside. Someone produced another bottle of hooch, and I waited with the Knights to have a drink.

"So is Madame Colet a Lady Knight? How exactly do you refer to her?" The liquor loosened my tongue that was already oiled up from all the speechifying. They all looked at the Sage.

"We embrace her as we embrace Mother Jones. They are women, but stronger than most men for the Cause." I am not sure who this Mother Jones is, but they all seemed to regard her as holy, maybe Camille as well. The Master Workman pulled me aside later as I walked to the exit.

"I don't know how close you have become with Madame Colet, but, as a man, I feel that I should tell you something." He came near enough for me to smell the whiskey on his breath. "The woman is not to be trifled with, my friend, if that is your intention. It is said that she put a pellet of something into Mayor Barret's glass at the inauguration party cutting his term from four years to four agonizing days." He clapped me on the back as I reentered the harsh daylight.

    I must admit that I looked at Camille a bit differently as we rode back to Vandeventer Place. In some ways, I have come to think of her as a poor, weak woman in need of my protection; however, I have witnessed a great store of strength lurking somewhere below the surface, more dangerous for being invisible. I don't believe the story about her poisoning the last Mayor or at least I don't want to. For her part, Camille seemed quite happy with the way I acquitted myself around her Union friends. She came to my room that night and called out my Christian name several times.

Chapter 26

ABIGAIL

I think I forgot something else that seems important. Madame Colet and Clara are very close. I don't remember exactly how they became so close, but they were always very friendly. One thing I remember was that not long after Madame became my teacher, she was summoned to the McPherson home quite urgently as one of the Germans maids who was with child had her time come while beating one of the rugs. Madame performed the duty of midwife as I sat in the drawing room reading *Sense and Sensibility*, a book about young women who seek husbands and children, though none of them shrieked like that poor German girl that day.

The screaming made me want to join in, but I managed to control it. The other thing I remember was that Madame had brought a small bottle of something called chloroform. She told me it was to help with the pain and was the same thing that Queen Victoria had used when she birthed the Prince of Wales. It was to be poured onto a handkerchief and placed over the nose of the person suffering, its dulling power simply inhaled.

The birthing took several hours. Eventually, the screaming was less frequent, and I moved to the top of the stairs near the room where it was happening. From there I could hear the German girl's heavy breathing and Clara's commanding voice giving orders while Madame spoke soothing words in German. Two servants came past me carrying some towels and a large bowl of steaming water. Sticking out of the bowl was a strange utensil that I had never seen before (Madame later told me they are called forceps). After the servants entered, they left the door open, so I could see inside. Clara shouted at them immediately.

"Wipe those dry with the towel, but don't touch them with your hand." She had removed her dress, and I could see her bloomers. Madame still wore her black servant's dress, but it had a darker sweat stain all across the back. I could only see the young girl from the side, her naked white legs trembling in a terrible rhythm. Madame washed her hands before gripping the forceps tightly.

"Hold her arms and say a prayer. It's time." The two servants complied while Clara poured some of the chloroform onto a rag and brushed it across the girl's face. I went down a few steps trying to remember a prayer I had heard when grandma and I used to go to church before the Catholics decided white and colored had to find God in separate buildings. Nothing would come to me.

"My dear God, help me!" The girl prayed for herself over and over until I heard Madame give out a great yell that was soon followed by the frightened cry of a babe suddenly alive. All of them shouted words that I could not understand or maybe they were not words. The servants eventually came out looking relieved and almost giddy as they hauled away the towels and a bloody sheet. I suppose they sent word to Mrs. Roberts, a woman who has survived giving birth to nine live children, as she soon plodded past me up the stairs. The old woman gave me a humorous look to imply that my time of lying in would be coming straight away.

Madame and Clara left the room soon after Mrs. Roberts entered to take charge of things. Before I could announce my presence, they plopped onto the velvet settee in the hallway. The two women were exhausted, and Madame had a large stain on the front of her dress that looked like blood. Clara held up the little bottle of chloroform and kissed it.

"Thank God for that." Madame said that as she tapped the bottle with her long finger. "And thank you, goddess, for being such a kind, capitalist woman." Clara laughed heartily.

"Don't speak so. You are just out of you mind from the ordeal." She poured some chloroform onto a cloth daubing it gently under Madame's nose.

"I'm hideous and filthy." Madame pointed to her soiled dress.

"Yes, we need to take this off and see if the Irish girls can get it clean. I think I have something you could wear home." They didn't speak for a while, and I could hear only their breathing until Clara spoke again. "Come to my boudoir and let me be the dress maid who waits on you."

Since Clara's bedroom was on the first floor, I slunk quickly down the stairs and back to the parlor. I don't know whether they cared that I had seen them being so close or what I really saw. The only thing that truly impressed me was my fond wish to have anyone speak to me in just the way they spoke that day, as if neither could do anything wrong. Oh, and I never want to birth a child.

Chapter 27

FERGAL

I woke up this morning with nothing particular needing to be done except meet with Niedringhaus and some German businessmen at what they call a Turnverein. That's this place where the Germans go to climb ropes and swing around these things called Indian clubs and generally work up a sweat doing nothing. A couple of the men were having trouble with an Irish gang and Niedringhaus thought I might calm things down. Then, I read the morning paper. I like the fellow who writes the local stories, but I didn't like this one.

Held to Answer
William Jones, a colored man, was arrested early this morning after Mrs. Mary Hook and her friend Mathilde Collins, both white women, accused him of unlawfully detaining them in the area of North Fifth Street for lewd purposes. Jones has been remanded to the City Jail and is being held without bond.

Big cities like Saint Louis may seem to be thousands of people just going about their business with little interest in what anyone else might be doing on the other side of town. This is true until it isn't. The fact that a Negro man had accosted two white women was the sort of news that people paid attention to. I sent a servant down to the Turnverein to tell Niedringhaus I had urgent business. I left my breakfast unfinished, woke up Monahan in the carriage house where he sleeps, and headed for the Four Courts Building down on Clark. Monahan had some problems getting his bearings and was none too keen about visiting a jail at all. When we got off the streetcar, I gave one of the Italian boys a penny for some hot walnuts, which settled him some.

I spent most of an hour talking to the turnkey, a very busy sergeant, and finally Captain Rohan, who happily accepted a tipple from my flask. None of them thought the two women were telling the truth, but they felt obliged to take Bill Jones into custody for such a serious offense. Although they had not begun to question him in the determined manner of the police department to obtain a confession, that appeared to be in the offing.

"Can you give me a couple of days before you start in on him?" I put a hand firmly on Rohan's big shoulder. "The Mayor thinks it would be prudent." That's another word Niedringhaus uses all the time that I think means "smart." The captain held out his cup for another taste.

"Yes, that could be done. The thing is, I don't believe the case will hold up in court. The Hook girl was lying, but she seemed quite comfortable doing it. The other one had not had the practice. The boys were pretty sure we could crack her like an egg." He was quite pleased with himself.

"Why don't you get to doing it then before this business gets out of hand?" He lit one of my cigars and blew a great plume of smoke toward the filthy ceiling.

"We could do that, but apparently this Miss Collins has slipped town."

"The hell you say."

"I do. Gone off to Cape Girardeau to visit some relative or other and won't be returning for a week."

"A week?"

"Yes, but I have my doubts that we will see the woman for many weeks, if at all. She appears to hail from those parts." He got a serious look that I was afraid of. "As to your real concern there has already been some solid citizens asking questions about how soon we would be hanging this fellow for accosting white women in their fair city."

"What did you tell them?"

"I told them the Saint Louis police had everything in hand, and we do." He blew more smoke out toward me. "Tell the Mayor that there will be no lynch mobs in Saint Louis that might disturb his great parade." I nodded to let him know that I understood his position. He would rather young Bill expire while trying to escape than have to deal with irate citizens, especially ones who were well-connected. He gave me all he knew about the supposed whereabouts of the Collins girl, and I grabbed Monahan and left with a heavy heart.

It was heavy for most of the wrong reasons, to be sure. I liked Bill Jones and knew he was getting railroaded, but I was more worried that it might come out that I had secured his position as a streetcar driver knowing full well that he was a colored man. Even though he was light-skinned enough to pass, and even though the laws on who can work what jobs are somewhat confusing of late, the fact of the matter is that I am responsible for him driving that streetcar. Damned luck.

I can find no way out of this problem after thinking on it all of the afternoon, and I have mostly given up. There is no train to Cape Girardeau, and the roads to there are treacherous, even worse with the recent rains having washed so many out. I am writing this early as Clara has invited me to a late supper. I will try to make it a light occasion though my heart is heavy.

Chapter 28

FERGAL

It is much better to be lucky than anything else. My father used to say that often, mostly to cast aspersions on those with industry or talent, and though I try not to live by the adage, it applied to me this day. First of all, when I told Clara last night my tale of woe, she was absolutely convinced that I needed to go to Cape Girardeau and fetch Mathilde Collins back to recant her story.

"It's 100 miles away at least on some of the worst roads in Missouri."

"Steamboat?"

"That would be easier, but I wouldn't get back in two days. By then Bill will take a bad fall or two, or sign some confession, and Mathilde won't matter one bit." As we discussed the matter, she was wearing only a black chemise and was firm about it staying in place until we had exhausted the subject.

"I know another way, the fastest way there is." She had a look of resolve, mixed with passion, and I knew I was done for.

It turns out that a Mrs. Worthington, our neighbor here in Vandeventer Place, has had a Mr. John Wise as a houseguest for the last month. Mr. Wise, it also turns out, is the world famous balloonist who is trying to raise money for, God help him, a great transcontinental flight. As she told the story, I slowly realized what the crazy woman was thinking.

"You mean fly in some contraption to Cape Girardeau? What fool would do such a thing." She laughed like a young girl.

"Nonsense. I used to go up in his balloon all the time back in '59 when he was planning to make his first historic flight. It's exhilarating!"

I suppose it was some combination of the urgency of the situation and my need to show Clara that I had no fear of something she had done many times, but I decided to do it. If she had not shown her appreciation of my courage so passionately later that evening, I might have changed my mind. In any event, this morning I went with Clara to Forest Park where this John Wise was setting up his damned balloon.

"Good morning, Clara. Good morning, sir." Wise pumped my hand as if I was some long lost cousin of his. He was a happy fellow, I'll attest to that, with all his gages and the great monster of a red and white blob growing ever larger behind him. When he told Clara that we would make much better time if she stayed behind, she pouted some until he gently kissed her hand which made me wonder how she came to have so much sway over the old man to get him to take this trip so suddenly.

I didn't dwell on that too much as I spent some time helping Wise with the bags of sand and baskets of provisions to be loaded. To be honest, I was trying to hurry things up before I lost my nerve entirely. Wise seemed glad that there was nary a cloud in the sky, and I was glad if he was. One of his two assistants handed us a map, which the man briefly consulted. Too briefly for my taste. Somehow, though I jumped into the little basket without changing my mind.

"Please don't die." Clara said that cheerful thing as the ropes were untied to free us from the bonds of this earth, and then the strangest thing happened. I died, or so it seemed, as I slowly floated upward leaving Clara McPherson in her big white hat and all the rest of the world, behind me. For just a moment, I thought it grand to see such a sight, to be so suddenly above the tallest trees in the park with no effort. But that exhilaration wore off quickly making me shortly want to grab John Wise by the neck and force him to take us back down to earth.

"First time up?" He wasn't looking at me as he messed about with this and that, but I think he could tell I was struggling.

"Yes."

"That's odd. Clara told me that you were an old hand at it. Said you were in the Balloon Corps during the War." He laughed. "She is such a panic, ain't she?"

"She is certainly a panic." About that time, I noticed my hands start to shake, and I took out a cigar to calm myself only to see it fly into the breeze after Wise slapped it out of my mouth.

"My God, man. You'll kill the both of us." He was quite distressed as he pointed upwards. "This gas making us weightless is hydrogen. The tiniest flame or even a spark would incinerate the balloon instantly in a huge ball of fire." Just then my shakes got a bit worse. I reached for the flask in my coat pocket.

"Damn me to Hell." In my hurry to ready myself at such an ungodly hour, I must have forgotten it. Wise appeared to understand my dismay and pulled a bottle out of one of the baskets of provisions.

"Amontillado? We have two of these if you care for some to take the chill off the morning." I did. Amontillado is too sweet for me under normal circumstances, but I was singing its praises this day.

Thus fortified, I did my best to enjoy the trip and the godlike view. Looking back at the great mess of smoke and soot that was Saint Louis, I felt proud to call it my home. It looked formidable and alive, a great beast manufactured from the minds of men. The rest of Missouri from where I was looking was mostly empty with all these farms scattered about between great square patches of nothing. The Mississippi looked grand snaking along the ground with its unstoppable force. Ballooning is not such a bad thing as long as the booze holds out.

"How fast are we going, would you say?" Saint Louis was getting smaller very quickly.

"All depends on the wind. On my great journey from Saint Louis to Henderson, New York, back in '59, I averaged over 40 miles an hour. I don't think we'll make that, but it will be a short trip."

"What was in Henderson, then?" I had never heard of the place and was surprised it would be a great destination.

"Nothing, really. That was just where we crashed due to an unfortunate squall." He began eating one of the loaves of bread he had brought. "These things happen." I finished the amontillado.

Eventually, Saints be praised, he went through the various gyrations to land the thing without killing us. There was a great field right next to the Normal School, and we slowly descended into it. A small crowd of young boys who had been watching us for a while cheered as we landed. I almost hit one with the anchor that Wise had me toss out. Even with what I thought was a good throw, we bumped a bit across the ground before it secured us.

I had some trouble getting out of the basket as it was still none too stable. I tossed coins to a couple of the bigger boys to help Wise get the balloon tied down and got directions to the address for Miss Collins that the police had given me. Walking there, a bit tipsy from drinking, and none too stable yet on solid ground, I was fairly certain that the whole foolish adventure had been for naught. Imagine my surprise, then, when a young woman answered the door of the old country house.

"Miss Mathilde Collins?" I spoke in an official way as I flashed the shiny badge the city gives me for working in the Mayor's office. I also let her see the revolver I had brought with me, the old one from my Tucson days that hasn't been fired in five years or cleaned in six. She started crying immediately without me having to use one harsh word.

"I'm so sorry. I didn't mean to say those things, but Mary made me swear to her story. She was stepping out on her husband and got scared because it was so late." She confessed to everything right there in what passed for a parlor. The old aunt, who must have been sixty if she was a day, just sat in a rocking chair while I made the girl write everything down and sign it. When she was done, I put the paper in my pocket and told her to follow me.

"How much trouble am I in?" Mathilde was only about nineteen or so and not as hard as so many of these Saint Louis women become without a man to take care of them or a family with money. I gave her one of my cards and told her that she had my protection for telling the truth, and she clenched it tightly. To be honest, I had a good notion to turn her over my knee and give her what Paddy gave the drum for risking a man's life, but I had something else in store for her.

"Your carriage awaits, m'lady." She gawked at the huge spectacle of the balloon. Wise had spread out a blanket and was having a picnic of sorts on the grass. Three or four of the country urchins were playing about in the basket until I boxed their ears and sent them packing. When Mathilde realized that she was to be a passenger, she began to sob at the thought of it. I gave her a stern look, and she accepted the situation though she was still terrified.

"Mr. Wise. Tell Clara to have my man Phelim Monahan accompany this young lady down to police headquarters along with this confession." I put the piece of paper into his jacket pocket. Together we cleaned up his little picnic and threw everything into the basket.

"Will you not be returning with us on this lovely day for flying about?" I like Wise well enough, but I hope never too see him or his balloon again.

"No, you said the extra weight could slow us down, and there is some urgency in this." I tipped my hat to Miss Collins before swooping her up and depositing her in the unsteady basket. She still sobbed, but made no great fuss. I turned to Wise. "If she falls out, don't lose that paper."

I untied the ropes myself and watched the great ship float away. The many screams of Miss Collins that began almost instantly slowly faded to resemble the song of a sad bird. I listened to them for a while before heading for the steamboat dock.

Chapter 29

ABIGAIL

The Veiled Prophet came to town just as everyone said he would, and he paraded through the streets of Saint Louis for all to see. Madame Colet had little interest in his arrival, but many, like Aunt Betha, were quite excited. Her Mr. Peck was the son of one of the "originals" which is what Father says the men paying for the celebration call themselves. My aunt had her seamstress make her a fantastic gown, all organza and feathers, for the Ball. I, of course, was not going. Even though at seventeen I could be considered a debutante, only very rich normal girls went to the Ball.

"Never you mind, *mon canard*. It will be a dreary affair with those poor girls just one more possession for their rich fathers to show off." For my part, I was excited about the parade. Even though he had official duties that day, as did father, Max had arranged for us to meet downtown for a part of the time.

After much discussion, it was decided that Madame and Mr. Monahan, the burly man who works for my father, would escort me to the riverfront. Madame did not complain and even fixed my hair in braids that made my felt bonnet with its pale blue ribbons look smart.

I also wore a walking dress with only a slight bustle and carried a white woolen stole. I was hoping Max might forgo his duties for me. Of the several times that we had seen one another since Clara's party, we had only managed a few stolen kisses, but I could tell he longed for more. As did I.

"Come along now. We don't want to miss this prophet." Madame caught me staring at myself in the mirror daydreaming. I felt sorry for her that she was wearing a plain, almost shabby plaid dress and an old straw hat. I felt even sorrier that my grandma, who would have loved the parade, would not be able to see it. I wonder if other people always think sad things at moments of happiness. Madame and I, followed by the lumbering Mr. Monahan, headed off for the streetcar, the crisp October air in our noses, while behind us the tired sun lost its grip on the sky as it sank into the dark.

The car was crowded by the time we got to Washington Square causing Madame to shoot an icy glance at Mr. Monahan that encouraged him to give up his seat to a woman and her young daughter. As we approached the Mississippi, the streets were crowded as well, and the noise of the many groups singing and shouting and laughing was like the calls of the birds in spring. The route of the parade was already lit with hundreds of Japanese lanterns while the riverfront blazed with the flames of a thousand torches. As we exited the streetcar, Mr. Monahan led the way, his wide body cutting a path into the crowd that we strolled through.

"Right here, ladies! You are just in time." Max, my dear Max, called to us from the corner of Walnut and Second Street where he had reserved a space for us. He was dressed in his beautiful grey wool suit, his derby tilted rakishly to one side. Shooing away the men who had been holding our seats, Max wiped off the chairs with his handkerchief. A band started playing "The Battle Hymn of the Republic" just as I took his hand in greeting. Madame seemed surprised I could touch him so easily without having a fit. I was rather smug, when I recall the moment. I didn't care what she or anyone else thought.

The parade began with twenty or so policemen in their bright blue coats marching down the street. They carried sabers, and though they had a serious look, one gave me a little smile and a wave as he went by. The theme of the parade had to do with the way that man's genius and perspicacity had given us the Modern World. Six horses pulled each float that had titles like "Wealth" and "Industry" painted on the sides. The goddess Ceres holding a stalk of corn was surrounded by her handmaids who tossed out sweets to the children in a bored manner. There was much, much more, but I only had eyes for Max as he watched the crowd for any problems.

"I see the Prophet. He has come as foretold." Some young man who had climbed up a lamp post for a better look announced that news, and, sure enough, there he was holding court on the very last float. Dressed in a light green robe with a great pointed hood over his head, the Veiled Prophet sat on a golden throne barely acknowledging the cheers of the crowd. My father must have had some influence on the outfit because the man did not look as terrible as the picture I had seen. Still, at the other end of his float a huge man held an axe and kept one foot on a chopping block. As the wagon passed in front of us a Negro man stepped out into the street holding up his hand. The horses hesitated.

"False Prophet! You do not own the streets of Saint Louis!" He seemed under the influence of spirits, and for a moment I wondered whether he might be part of the show. Max did not think so, and he was already on his feet with his cane in his hand. Before he could even take three steps, a policeman struck the back of the man's head with a club twice before jerking him out of the way of the advancing float. The man tried to return to the street, only to be struck again, this time by several men in the crowd. When I realized that they might kill him on the spot, I began to scream with such force that the Prophet raised up from his chair to locate the source of the racket.

"Constable House, secure that man and take him to the Hoosegow!" Max, who seemed to know the policeman, had stopped in his tracks when I started screaming. After giving his order, he returned to my side looking unsure of what to do next. I collapsed into his arms while Madame Colet gently tapped my back.

"Please escort her home, Mr. Niedringhaus. I believe Abigail has seen enough of this parade today." I was still sobbing despite my efforts to control myself.

"Yes, of course. My carriage is just around the corner." His voice was very soothing as he held me firmly, but with a gentleness.

They decided that Max and I, accompanied by Mr. Monahan, should leave while Madame would follow the two police officers who were conducting the Negro man off to jail to make sure that no harm came to him. Just how she intended to do that, I was unsure. On the way back through the crowd, we found Mr. Monahan leaning against the side of the bank building in a poor state of health. His eyes were glassy, and some drool ran from the corner of his mouth. Max directed me away from the man without a word. After a short walk, we came upon the little carriage where it waited in a vacant lot. Max spoke to the driver who put out his cigar as soon as he saw us.

"Up to Vandeventer Place, but take it slow. This young woman has taken ill." The driver gave me just the right look of pity as Max helped me into the rig.

"It will be slow going anyway, sir, with this crowd."

I have always loved being inside a coach. Even with all the noise still going outside, I felt quite snug inside, and most of my hysterics passed. I asked Max to close the leather curtains as the light was bothering me.

He did so as if he believed me, but I don't truly think he did. With the world mostly shut out, I took his dear face in my hands knocking off the derby that he had yet to remove. We came together for a kiss as if that was the most natural thing to be doing.

"Are you sure that you are quite yourself, Abbie?" The kiss had lasted a good while, and Max breathed like a man who had just run up a steep hill.

"I am sick of being myself, being some silly young girl." I grabbed a handful of his hair and kissed him again with all the passion in my life. "I want to be the woman that you have awakened." To be honest, I did not think of those words in the moment, but it was a speech I had thought about for many days. It affected him greatly, and his hands began to touch me in new and thrilling places.

"*Liebchen!*" Max began to speak in German saying many things I did not understand. Still, those hard consonants and umlauted vowels excited me almost as much as what his fingers were doing. The anatomy lessons that Madame and Clara had given stood me in good stead as my own hands, moving without shame, began to explore the physical presence of my heretofore Platonic love. The buttons on his trousers were many, but my hands were remarkably steady in their undoing although I think I tore a stubborn one. I felt my walking dress slide easily up my legs leaving only a petticoat and knickers left to defend me, and I quickly discarded those.

"*Ich liebe dich.*" I said this before kissing him again. He was staring at my bare legs as if they were some treasure that he had just discovered. The carriage was clopping on cobblestones, and even going slowly, it bounced about making our embraces seem to shake the very earth beneath us.

"*Mein Mann!*" I think that may have been incorrectly said, but we were creating a new logic of grammar in the moment. Max seemed suddenly confused, even as he grasped my knee tightly. Luckily, my conversation with Clara regarding the ways of an amorist came back to me just in time. She had mentioned that a woman in love could "mount" a man, much as I mounted my dear horse Silver Dollar in Bellefontaine. So I did. Max was a bit taken aback, but warmed to the concept very quickly. I did as well, and the pain the Clara had warned me about, though real, was a small thing. Outside the oasis of our carriage, fireworks for the parade began their loud pops and flashes. They would have once terrified me, but now they were nothing, just a little noise that faded as we slowly drew ever closer to Vandeventer Place and home.

By the time the driver announced our arrival, we were both spent as I lay me head on his shoulder. I continued to whisper in his ear, but he was mostly silent as he rearranged his clothing. I did the same before the driver opened the carriage door. Max exited first to help me down, declining my invitation to come inside as he had to return to the parade. Although I could not understand the odd look on his face, I took that as a part of my inability to understand what other people are feeling, especially men. I was not worrying about it, though. I was happy, more than happy; I was fulfilled.

Chapter 30

FERGAL

Well, that was a time. I have not been able to write for several days as there has been too much to do. The parade went off without a hitch, and the fall weather was quite crisp and beautiful for marching about for no good reason. I didn't get to see a lot of it as I was preoccupied with a small disturbance on Biddle with the Irish. Of course, many of the young ones take any excuse to get drunk, and a parade is as good as any for disturbing the peace. I paid a bunch of Egan's Rats to thump the four or five troublemakers who refused my appeals to Reason, and that did the trick. I made sure those boys did not become too passionate about the thumping so I'm fairly certain most of those dumb Micks were only missing a tooth or three the next day.

Later that evening, the parade committee met on the rooftop of Tony Faust's, and Claymore stood rounds for me and Niedringhaus to express his appreciation for a job well done. Most of the swells left early to get ready for the ball where the Veiled Prophet was to select the Queen of Love and Beauty. Addison was nowhere to be seen which was fine by me. Niedringhaus was in a somber mood, and I was wondering how many heads he had busted downtown on the parade route. Sensing the need for cheer, Claymore slapped our backs to begin a speech.

"Gentlemen, we have done a great thing today. We have started a new tradition in Saint Louis that will last for centuries after we have shuffled off of this mortal coil." He went on like that, speaking like a politician, for a good while with much additional backslapping and ordering of booze. The little band started playing some German songs, and I thought Niedringhaus's mood might be improving. I was wrong.

As soon as he and I left the party to attend to one more task, he pulled a long face. Our particular duty, which was supposed to be a reward for all of our hard work, was to be an easy one (I was hoping it didn't replace the hard cash that had been promised). At about seven o'clock, the two of us strolled across the street to the Planter's Hotel with the intention of assuming the great honor of escorting the Veiled Prophet to the ball.

"I wonder if we'll get to stay at this party for the free drinks." I put an arm around Niedringhaus as we got to the door of the hotel. He removed his hat to run his hand through his hair,

"I need to talk to you about Abigail. There's been a terrible misunderstanding." I cut him off.

"There is no understanding women at all, my friend. Whatever fool thing my daughter has said to you, she doesn't mean it. Don't trouble yourself."

"But-"

"Nothing more about it." To be sure, I had some apprehension about his friendship with a girl as troubled as Abigail, but I didn't want to hear about it on such a festive night. "Let's just get this bum to the ball. A young man like yourself might find a debutante or two there."

There was a group of policemen in the hotel lobby looking miserable with their uniforms all pressed and even sporting white gloves for the occasion. They nodded at us as we went by. Slayback was just coming out the door dressed in a gray suit with a fancy top hat when we entered the hallway. He greeted us warmly enough for a swell. I suppose he was thrilled at the way his idea had come to life.

"Good evening, gentlemen! The Prophet is almost ready to select the queen." We stood there, neither of us knowing what to say to such nonsense. He changed his tone back to wealthy man about town. "By the way, Addison has been dismissed as of this afternoon. He was a little too light-fingered with the parade funds, and I won't tolerate that." I couldn't tell if he was giving me good news or a warning about all the money he imagined that I'd purloined. I nodded without smiling, and we went into the hotel room.

The Prophet was in his underwear shaving. Police Commissioner Priest, as I knew him, acknowledged us with the briefest of waves. His robes and great hood were scattered on the bed like the skin shed by an animal. I was fascinated by how the heavy gold drapes seemed almost solid in their opulence and how deeply my boots sank into the dark green rug. Niedringhaus, still in a poor mood, asked if he would prefer us to wait outside.

"No. I'll only be a moment. I may take the hood off later to reveal myself to the crowd, and I want to look my best." About then there was a knock on the door. Niedringhaus answered it and got punched in the nose for his trouble. The fellow who did the punching pushed his way in striking poor Max a second time and knocking him to the floor. It was that bastard Addison carrying a cavalry sword in one hand, a small revolver in the other. He slammed the door behind him and faced me with great hatred in his eyes. In an instant I understood that he knew I had ratted on him and was drunk enough to kill me for it.

"Don't be a damned fool, man." The Commissioner was trying to be in charge of the situation which is difficult for any man in his skivvies.

"There are five officers of the law in the lobby who would take great pleasure in beating you to a pulp. I suggest you leave now and catch the first train out of town."

"You Yankee scum telling all your vile calumny and filthy lies about me. I will send you and the rest of them to Hell this day. I have -"

I could tell he was none too happy with me and wanted to get a few things off his chest, so I took a chance while he was railing and swung my cane at the hand holding the gun. I caught him square on the forearm knocking it to the carpeted floor. He screamed and came at me swinging his sword like a madman possessed by the Devil himself. I think only the fact that he was as drunk as a fiddler saved me from being slashed, not my fighting skills.

"Damn!" The Commissioner cursed away behind me and scrambled to get something from off the bed. I was hoping that it was a Colt .44, but it turned out to be a silver police whistle. Before he could blow it though, Addison, who realized the implications of such an action, threw his saber at the poor man's head, the hilt landing right between his eyes. At the same time, the scoundrel leapt for the gun on the floor. I froze, not sure whether to try to get out the window or hope the gun would jam.

Neither of those things happened as Niedringhaus, suddenly recovered, smacked Addison in the head with what looked to be a thin shoe or something made of leather. Turns out it was a sap filled with a nice, thick piece of lead. The first blow caused Addison to forget about the gun. The second made him forget his name. These Germans may go on and on about Hegel or whoever, but when the situation calls for it, they can be as vicious as the meanest Mick in a dark alley. I put the boot into Addison's ribs a few times for good measure.

"I think the Commissioner needs some medical attention." Niedringhaus, whose nose was bleeding heavily, was looking at the unconscious Priest's forehead that was already sprouting a great egg. He held one of the man's eyes open and listened to his chest.

"He's just cold-cocked. He'll come around in a few hours." I walked over behind him, the gun safely in my hand. "Thanks for saving my life, by the way." The German was thinking and acted as if he'd not heard me.

"You're going to have to put on these robes and play the Prophet." He held them up to me. "You're about the same height as Priest, and no one will know anything if you don't take off the hood."

I argued some, but he was right. Claymore and the Mayor wanted the ball to go off as planned. I gave Niedringhaus my damned silk handkerchief to press on his nose and picked up the robes. Just then Addison somehow came to life and took off out the door. I looked at Niedringhaus with a question in my eyes that he answered.

"Let him run. We'll get him later if he doesn't hop the next train for California. There's too much to be done."

By the time I got all trussed up like some fool potentate, the cops were knocking on the door. Niedringhaus answered to tell them that Mr. Dunne had taken ill all of a sudden, and he was staying with me. He told the two sergeants to take our places as escorts, but that nobody should say a word to the Commissioner on the way as he was in a most foul temper.

So it came to pass that an Irishman of no social standing at all became the Veiled Prophet. I rode in the fancy open carriage to the Merchant's Exchange with cops in front and behind me. I waved graciously to the people who gawked on the street as if I was above everything. The costume helped me much with the ruse, but when no one was looking, I stuck my flask under that veil for additional fortification.

"Ladies and Gentlemen! A great Prophet has arrived from the far-off land of Khorassan, a place of infinite wonder and elegance. Tonight, he will not only grace us with his royal presence, but will select a queen from the great beauties of Saint Louis assembled in the great hall. Huzzah!" That announcement and a whole lot of other mumbo-jumbo was shouted out to the crowd when I arrived, and everyone cheered like I was the Pope, himself. I strode slowly across the ballroom, having a hard time seeing through the veil, nodding at all the swells in their fancy duds as I went. There were more diamonds on the ladies, rings, necklaces, tiaras, than I had ever seen, but they all curtsied nicely to a dumb Mick who was more than a little in his cups.

In one corner, there was a golden throne, wood to be sure, but painted gold and dandied up quite nicely. I took my place upon it for more silly speeches and music that seemed played to put a man to sleep. I think I did doze for a minute or two. When I opened my eyes beneath the veil, young women were parading themselves toward me, pretty as you please.

"Miss Emily Bain," some fellow called out as a winsome young thing approached my throne in a pale blue gown. Her waist was cinched so tight that I think I could have circled it completely with just my two hands. Poor Miss Bain looked as if she might pass out from lack of air. She came quite close to allow me to study her pretty, though a bit horsey, face, and I wondered if she was aware that her dear father had legalized the whoring for a few years in Saint Louis. I think not.

"Miss Susie Slayback!" Luckily, Claymore had informed me that Slayback's daughter, a very pert and confidant young girl, was to be chosen the Queen of Love and Beauty. She was pretty enough, but a little too sure of herself for my taste. If I'd taken one more pull from the flask that evening, I swear before all that is holy that she would have gone home without being queen of anything. The only thing I did was to give her chubby cheek a good pinch when she presented herself before my grandness, just to see the shock on her rich face.

Ah, I picked her anyway, and the dancing started. Most of it was the fancy waltzing, which the youngsters must have been practicing because they did it so well, though I would have preferred a good jig or at least a reel. At some point, it was decided that the Prophet needed to begin his journey back to Khorassan, his work of bringing joy and light to the city having been completed. Everyone cheered as I again walked very slowly through the crowd waving my hand as if I was casting a spell or giving a blessing. Just as I came up to the exit, I noticed one Stephen Peck, my sister's dull fiancé, making an elaborate bow in my direction. I stopped to play with my veil so I could see better. Just next to him, all got up in a white and silver gown that must have covered a formidable pile of crinoline was my dear sister Betha. As she struggled to curtsy without causing her corset to explode, I stopped and placed a hand on her bowed head.

"Dear child, what is your name?" I used the eerie voice that I employ for telling ghost stories. She replied without daring to raise her eyes to my greatness.

"Betha Tidd."

"Tidd? That is not an Irish name. There is a lilt in your voice of the Old Sod."

"My family name was Dunne, your majesty." She wasn't sure how to address someone as important as me and sounded as nervous as a whore in Church. I leaned in close to her ear and whispered in my normal voice.

"Don't you forget it, colleen." I could tell she recognized me from the way she jumped. "And loosen up your corset some and have yourself a good fart."

That was how I exited the hall with no one but my dear sister the wiser. I climbed back into my fancy carriage and was driven slowly back to the Planter's House where Niedringhaus and Claymore awaited my arrival. The poor Commissioner had been carted off to City Hospital, but he will be fine, I'm told. The three of us celebrated into the wee hours of the morning, which is why I am writing this one day late. They deposited me in Vandeventer Place as the sun was just starting to warm up the Mississippi, and I didn't stir until late afternoon, then only to eat a bit before going back to bed. I suppose the Veiled Prophet can name his own hours.

Chapter 31

ABIGAIL

The Veiled Prophet came and went. Father and Max were involved in the fancy ball where the Queen of Love and Beauty was selected from the richest debutantes. As I lolled around the house for the next several days, I felt as if I had had already been transformed into that Queen forever. I assiduously applied myself to my German lessons with Madame secretly longing to tell her my secret, that I was truly beloved. On the other hand, my good fortune made me too magnanimous to brag to the poor woman, who was an old widow (she was 35!) with no romantic prospects at all.

"You seem to have recovered well from your illness at the parade, my girl." Madame could sense something. She was very intuitive, but I only grinned like the little girl I had been a few days earlier and went back to learning my dative prepositions.

"*Aus, ausser, bei, mit, nach, seit, von, und zu.*" That is all there are. Unfortuately, so many other prepositions are both dative and accusative depending on their use in a sentence. (I know I'm being a fool, but I want to delay telling this next part.)

My little state of bliss did not last very long. I did not hear from

Max for many days, too many days for something to not be something amiss. After a week I could feel myself sinking into a state similar to when my grandma died, when the world seemed about to end for me, and no one cared. If only I had told Madame, things might have been less terrible, but I did not. I just sulked. Madame seemed to be spending many hours with Clara and let me have my way. At some point, I found myself reverting to my old habit of lying under the dining room table curled up in a ball. One morning as I was so reposed, my aunt's shrill voice broke through my reverie, but she was not speaking to me.

"I need a word with you, brother, if you've the time for me." Her slippered feet and the hem of her robe were all I could see below the tablecloth. My father approached from behind my head, and they both sat down.

"Do you still have your Irish up about the ball? I was only having a bit of fun with you."

"I don't give one tinker's damn about the Veiled Prophet or whatever you men think up to amuse yourselves." Her feet twitched as she spoke. "There are some serious things that need discussing between us."

"Fire away, sister dear." My father has been in a very good mood since the Veiled Prophet celebration and seemed to be feeling quite brotherly. My aunt sniffed as if she were not yet convinced of his good will.

"Stephen and I have set a wedding date in January."

"Such a cold month to become Mrs. Peck." My aunt's foot began to twitch even more. "And such a short engagement. People might talk." He meant this to be a joke, I think, but she found no humor in it.

"It's a tradition in his family to marry at the beginning of the year or some nonsense." There was silence for a while, and it is possible that he took her hand.

"Congratulations, sister. Do you get along with his fancy Saint Louis family?" My aunt laughed in a cynical way.

"Well enough. His mother, thank the Lord, is already in the grave. She would have been a terror from the stories I've been told. The father just cares that I turn out well in the proper duds and keep my pretty mouth mostly shut." My father said something I could not hear. My aunt's reply was curt. "That's why I need you to hold some greenbacks for me."

They talked a long time about money. My aunt feared that upon marrying Mr. Peck her considerable fortune would come entirely under his control allowing her husband and master to decide whatever amount of "pin money" might be allotted to her every month. In case of some emergency, she wanted my father to hold ten thousand dollars that she would transfer to him before the wedding. The good news for me was that she would let us rent the house at a very reasonable price so that we wouldn't have to move somewhere new.

"So you'll be going to his house in Soulard, then?" My father started using the voice of a politician, friendly, but practical.

"For a time. Stephen wants to build a house near the new County seat out west. It seems that he bought up some land from that Hanley fellow when he was betting on the separation from the City."

"The County! There's nothing out there except pigs and chickens, and that's probably all there will ever be. You'll be miserable."

"A wife goes where her husband says." If I didn't know my aunt was speaking above me, I would have thought she was on the verge of tears. She shook her emotions off to go on. "There's something else you need to know. About Abigail."

"Abigail? What's she done?" I felt the blood rush to my head when my father immediately thought I had done wrong in some way. My aunt lowered her voice, but I could still hear her.

"I was approached yesterday by your friend Niedringhaus's Aunt Gertrude, a Prussian woman who claims to be descended from royalty of whatever sort they have over there."

"I met her once. Formidable woman."

"Yes, since his parents passed, she and her husband have been treating him like the son they never had."

"And?" My father was struggling to hold on to his politician's voice, but he was losing. The topic of me worried him.

"It seems that a few night ago, after the parade, your dear companion, that you begged to befriend your dim-witted daughter, gave that same girl the burning shame in the back of his carriage." No sentence ever spoken has affected me so deeply. The coarse reference to what occurred was terrible enough, but the suggestion that my father had asked Max to "befriend" me wounded me to my core. I wished to stop my ears before hearing more. I did not.

"No wonder the poor man has been acting so queerly around me for these last few days." My father denied nothing that my aunt had said. "So what does the Prussian harpy want you to do? Keep me from thrashing him?"

"That doesn't seem to have crossed her mind, though she does want to protect her poor nephew and make sure that he is not forced into an unacceptable marriage." My aunt's foot was perfectly still. "She has heard that the girl is both of mixed blood and weak mind, and she will accept no obligation that anyone in her family will have to marry her under any circumstances." My father took a deep breath.

"Is that how Niedringhaus feels as well?"

"It appears so. He came crying to his aunt about how your Abigail ravaged him like a cat in heat in a way that made him fear for his life."

"Impossible. She's but a girl who knows nothing of such things."

"You could be right, and the old woman may have been saying those things to scare me. That could be true enough. Nevertheless, I knew a young whore once who couldn't make an X to sign her name, but was a genius at ripping up the sheets. It could be the savage blood in your daughter that's turned her wrong."

"There's more Irish blood in her than anything else." I suppose that was my father's way of defending me. "What does this Gertrude want from us?"

"As I said, for us not to raise any Cain about Abigail being soiled by her nephew. She will keep him away from her forever in return." The last words each stabbed me straight in the chest. I do not understand how I remained silent.

"Done." The word, spoken by my father, was the final stab to my heart.

"I told her you would agree to those terms."

"Did you now." My father was angry, but not at her. "What's to be done with that girl?"

"You need to do something if you ever want to remarry."

"Adeline Crain was willing to accept her." My aunt blew air through her lips in a crude way.

"For a moment she was to get you to the altar. She told me that she had plans to send the girl to be shut up with the nuns, and you should consider that yourself. Abigail is nothing but a stone around your neck."

That was the last thing they said before taking their leave of one another. I lay under the table for a long time, not crying, because tears did not seem sufficient. They were going to take everything in my life from me, and there was nothing I could do about it. No tears could wash that away. When I finally crawled out to go upstairs, I decided that maybe I was wrong. Maybe there was something that a mad girl could do, that only a mad girl would do.

Chapter 32

ABIGAIL

I am sorry to tell this part of the story, but I cannot stop now. I stayed in my room the rest of the afternoon refusing dinner or to be comforted by Madame who spoke to me very kindly, but was only a servant with no power. I counted the lines on my hands over and over as I used to do feeling myself slowly becoming nothing, the nothing I was born to be. I had to do something, something to decide my fate once and for all. That was how I, in my self-importance, thought of my actions, as if I were Antigone about take an action from which there was no return. Maybe we all are once.

I sent a note to Max. This was not easy to do while keeping it secret, but I managed to give it to the Thornton boy along with a whole silver dollar and the strict instructions to hand it to Mr. Niedringhaus personally. The letter read something like this (I kept no copy):

Dearest Max,

I know that many are attempting to persuade you to abandon our love. I understand the concerns of your family and friends who want you to be happy in this Life. In their eyes I will only be a great burden to you with my tainted blood and queer mind. Still, I believe that your affection for me is real; I know it in my heart. You must also know in your heart of my great love for you. Because of that love I will abide by any decision you make regarding my hopes. If you choose never to see me again, I will accept your wish and become a ghost to you, but I will be a ghost that loves you forever,

Abigail Dunne

It is impossible to express my excitement when I received a response just a day later. The Monahan girl brought it to me with what might have been a wry smile on her face. I'm afraid that I was a bit cross with her for such impertinence saying something about minding her business if she wanted to continue her employment in the house. (My association with Clara has had some effect on me, not all good, I fear.) She went away with downcast eyes, but my distress was great as I held the small envelope. A reply so fast was not necessarily a good thing; I was half expecting it to be a farewell letter.

Much to my great joy, it was not. The small envelope contained a scribbled note requesting me to meet my dear Max that very night at the entrance to Forest Park at eleven o'clock and come away with him. It was signed with only an odd looking M, but I was so excited that details made no difference to the import of the words. I read the words over and over out loud until I almost put myself into a fit. There were only twenty of them, but they seemed better than a thousand written by any poet. My love had summoned me.

I spent the rest of the afternoon in my room mostly just staring at the ceiling reciting the words from the note over and over Madame asked me whether I wanted to come to Clara's house to learn about plants in her vast garden. I claimed to have a Wilkie Collins novel that I longed to finish. She looked confused as I had no such book near me (or anywhere in the house), but she went on her way without another word. I did not dine with the family that evening complaining of a stomach ailment. In truth, I was simply too excited to eat or be in the presence of any humans who were not Max Niedringhaus. When I was certain that all had retired for the night, I got up and prepared myself brushing my hair over and over until it shone. I dressed myself in my finest frock which was the one I had worn on Veiled Prophet day (I hoped Max would not notice or maybe I hoped he would). If Madame had come in to speak to me, I am certain that she would have learned everything, so near madness was I in my preparations. To keep myself from thinking of the consequences of my running away, I only concentrated on the moment I would see my dearest love letting all the other moments dwindle to nothing.

It was easy enough to get out of the house at around half past ten without being seen or heard. My only fear was running straight into Father, who had been out conducting city business and might come in at any time, but he did not. The October night was still warm for Saint Louis rendering the little shawl I had donned quite sufficient. Of course, I would not have cared if a blizzard was raging through the city, so passionate was my gait. I apologize for having to tell the next part of the story, but I can see no way around it. My hands tremble as I write making the ink pool into indecipherable blobs. I hope it makes sense.

The entrance to Forest Park on Kingshighway is not very fancy or well-lit. I was happy that I encountered no other person on my brisk walk there, but I was too foolish to feel any fear on my journey. When I arrived, I began to worry that I might have been confused about the exact meeting place. I also agonized about what time it was as I had no way of knowing. These were the only thoughts in my silly head when a man came out of the park and walked toward me.

"Do you have the time, please, sir?" I remember being quite pleased with myself for uttering those words without a single stutter, but that was the last moment I was pleased that night with anything. In a second, Hell opened its gates.

"Yes, you poor idiot. It is time for you to suffer for the sins of your father despite what the Bible says." I recognized the man then as Mr. Addison who had visited our home once. His face was red and he held a huge knife very close to my nose. He grabbed one of my arms before I could think of anything to say while another man who emerged from the shadows took the other arm and led me easily into the park.

It had not occurred to me how absolutely dark the place was at night as I had only been there on walks with Madame when all was bright and gorgeous. That night every tree was a twisted ghoul, each bush a crouching demon. Although the men told me several times to be silent, I fell into babbling incoherently. The other man, who was much larger than Addison, shook me until I stopped, but after a minute, I started again.

"I said hush, girl!" The big man said this right before he slapped me across the face. In my whole life, no one had ever hit me that hard, and it changed me instantly. I was no longer a young woman with a name and thoughts and feelings. I had been reduced to the basest of living things, a thing without a soul. I let them drag me to a clearing where Mr. Addison came very close to my face as he spoke.

"You are a maiden, I trust?" I could smell the whiskey on his breath as his beard scratched my nose.

"Yes." I was simply trying to say what he wanted to hear. I had some foolish idea that they might allow me to leave if I agreed with them.

"A maiden who sends love letters to a German bastard, whose messenger sells that letter to me." He began stroking my cheek tenderly, but there was no tenderness in the man. "This allowed me to lure you here like an innocent little lamb, a lamb who might be slaughtered if she gives us any trouble."

"Let me g-g-g." I pleaded with them as they began to handle me quite roughly, touching me in disgusting ways. My voice was too loud, I suppose, and the big man punched me very hard in the stomach knocking me to my knees. That seemed to please them to have me at their feet like some slave girl. Mr. Addison grabbed a handful of my hair, and told me to repeat certain phrases, vile ones about myself. To my shame, I admit that I did say some of them although my stuttering became too pronounced and he was not satisfied. Perhaps the worst part of the ordeal was not the physical and moral pain, but how much pleasure the men took in my suffering. I was just a puppet for them to enjoy.

"Abigail?" To hear my Christian name spoken at that moment just as my name was about to be erased from this world forever was a great joy. I said the name myself, the name my mother had given me, the name of the second first lady of America, just to hear it again. The two men growled, but that was drowned out by the loud crack of a pistol followed by a dull thud as a bullet met the trunk of the big man. The force of it twisted his torso like the invisible hand of a giant before he fell to the ground. Addison, reaching for the knife in his coat received a shot in his right shoulder bathing my face in his blood. He took a few steps backward until he fell rolling in pain. When my understanding returned, I saw Madame Colet, wearing her light jacket over her dressing gown, give an ivory handled pistol to Aiofe Monahan, who stood beside her.

"Give me your hand." Madame Colet said those words before pulling me to my feet. I allowed her to do that, but I think that I was not truly Abigail yet, but still that lower form of life filled with dread. There were words in my head that would not form in my mouth. Aoife stepped over to where the two men had fallen.

"You remember me, Addison? The whore with only one ear?" I think Mr. Addison started to reply to those questions in an uncouth fashion which was cut short when the Monahan girl fired into his chest. As the big man tried to sit up, she blasted him as well. I believe she might have shot yet again, but Madame grabbed her by the thin coat and pulled both of us away.

"We need to leave them alone to die before the coppers come." She took the pistol away from Aiofe and put it in the cloth bag that hung from her shoulder. We walked swiftly out of the park, not slowing down until we were a block up from Kingshighway.

"I'm so sorry, Madame." I cried into the sleeve of her walking dress as all my sorrow pulled the tears from my eyes. She kissed the top of my head.

"I hope you are not sorry for those brutes. I saw them strike you before I knew it was you for certain." She patted my swelling cheek. "Not that it mattered. They deserved what they got."

We did not speak again all the way back to Vandeventer Place. I watched Madame replace the revolver in Mr. Monahan's holster as he continued to sleep soundly in the sway of the opium he bought in Hop Alley. Only later in my bedroom did she feel the desire to talk.

"So you understand that it is best for you to never tell anyone about this?" She was very serious, and I nodded my head quickly. Then she explained how Aiofe had heard me reciting the words of the forged note and come to her, and how they followed me at a discrete distance after I sneaked out of the house. "I suppose I should have just stopped you, but I thought there might be a chance that this German had both a heart and a backbone."

"It wasn't his fault." I still needed to defend Max. She tossed her head.

"Do you know why those men sought you out?"

"It had something to do with Father." She gave me an odd look. Only then did I tell her about my father and aunt's conversation, about my doomed love for Max, about my hatred of the world. That hatred became even more pronounced as I felt the side of my face begin to swell from the blow I had received. Madame had brought a basin of water to the bed and was gently wiping the mud from my hands doing each finger at a time.

""Yes, the world of men can make a woman despair. Those brutes tonight were only somewhat less subtle about the way we are shoved to our knees to be brood mares without a complaint." She began to wash Mr. Addison's blood from my face.

"Madame, I know I am a great burden." I was surprised that I felt none of the usual discomfort at being touched.

"You are no burden at all, child." She thought a minute. "Fergal will put you nowhere without my approval, *mon fille*. You must not think of such a thing." I was surprised. I knew my father appreciated her as a servant, but I was surprised that she had so much confidence in her powers. I was also shocked that she had used his Christian name. "And this business with Max will be fixed" she snapped her fingers, "or he does not deserve any more of your love."

"But, Madame, I cannot imagine life without him."

"Better always to worry about giving love than what you get back." She gently brushed my hair, which was full of thistles and grass. "The world is a cruel place, especially for women. But if you are loved for a moment, you must cherish that and keep it as a balm against all the pain that will surely come." She hugged me gently for a long time. "There. Take my love and hold it forever."

I cried again, but more from joy than from pain. Although my face throbbed and hurt worse every second, I did not care.

Dear Reader, you must be thinking that this is a terrible account of the evening. When I reread it, I must agree. My mind went so many places during those hours that the truth of them eludes me. I apologize for my inept storytelling, yet I am glad to have Madame Colet's words conquer that memory.

Chapter 33

FERGAL

All my life I have known how fast things can change. When I was very young, I lost a little brother on the crossing from Ireland to America; one minute I was talking to him about some childish thing, and the next the fever took him, and I could never talk to him again. We all try to fool ourselves with some idea of permanence, of roots, but the deepest roots mean little if a tree is struck by a bolt of lightning. I was just struck today by a whole storm, and I write this in a kind of shock.

The day started out well enough. I received more praise for my performance at the ball from men in the know. I learned that Frank Addison had been found shot through the heart in Forest Park along with one of his cronies. The police, probably on orders from the Commisioner, won't look too closely into who did what. I even collected a decent little bonus from the Mayor by way of Claymore which I placed in my strongbox after counting the whole pot of gold three times. Even Betha has come to treat me like her dear brother, mostly because she needs my help holding money for her, but at least she remembers that she is my sister. I suppose I was concerned about this business with Abigail and

Niedringhaus, but that seems minor now in comparison to these new developments..

It's been several days since the Veiled Prophet went back to Khorassan which was supposed to allow me to return to the easy business of helping the Mayor run the city. Tonight, as it happened, I was invited by note to a late supper at Clara's house. I had not seen her in over a week, and I got a shave and a haircut at the Planter's house for the occasion. Madame Colet was nowhere to be seen as I left the house, which I thought to be a good thing at the time. On the short walk I remembered thinking that these days of my love affair with Clara were numbered, and the number was a low one. Still, I was a man with connections who could just walk away from any female problems that arose. I was still thinking something like that when Madame Colet answered the door at Clara's. I almost crapped my pants.

"Were you expecting someone else, Fergal?" Because she never called me by my Christian name in public, the sound of it added to the considerable shock I was feeling in that moment.

"Madame Colet. I did not know that you were visiting Mrs. McPherson as well." I was trying to judge the odd look on her face, which was like the cat that ate the canary. "Or are you betimes working for Mrs. McPherson now?" I was trying to remember some conversation about midwife services when I heard Clara's voice from behind her.

"I would never presume to hire Camille in any capacity." I could see the Lady of the house behind her in the foyer then. "She and I only collaborate as equals." Although the women did not laugh out loud, they seemed about to, and they were quite pleased with themselves. I went into the house though I considered turning around to head for the nearest tavern. We went to the small drawing room next to Clara's bedroom, and I saw not one servant in the place.

"Let's have a drink, shall we?" Camille acted as if she was the mistress of the house taking my arm to lead me to one of the mahogany chairs. I thought maybe the women would just have a dash of sherry, but we all had a couple of fingers of bourbon from that crystal decanter. I drank mine directly. Although I had never seen the French woman drink any spirits at all, she seemed familiar with it. Then Clara started in.

"Dear Fergal. There are many things that have been hidden that need to be out in the open. My mother always said that sunlight is a great cure." I shook my head.

"With all due respect, sunlight is not good for everything. Too much of it has been known to kill the healthiest of living things." Camille took ahold of my hand. I was tempted to pull away, but she had a grip of iron.

"Fergal, *mon cher*." She started in just that way. I looked at Clara who showed me nothing except the mere trickle of a smile. "We came to an understanding, Clara and I, about you some time ago, and it seems foolish not to be open about it, especially with you." I stood up all at once causing Camille to release my hand.

"Have you women lost your damned minds?" I was in a hurry to assert myself to this foolishness, the way someone of my stature usually did. "I don't know what modern books you have been reading, but any choices about such things are still up to me as a man."

"Fergal. Just listen." Clara was speaking to me in a tone that suggested I was a half-wit, and she got my Irish up.

"At this time with one of you in my employment and the other a married woman, I will probably choose to forget about the both of you and go on about my business as I see fit." I said that loud enough to cow them, but neither of them seemed to be cowed. Clara spoke right up.

"My marriage to Mr. McPherson is well on the way to being dissolved. The final papers have been submitted and a judge will be signing them within a week." She said this with no emotion in her voice.

"That's a scandalous thing you are doing."

"I'm comfortable with what men say is scandalous." She looked into my eyes as if we were alone. "Would you like to know the grounds for divorce?"

"I don't give a damn about any grounds at all." I had every intention of leaving them in that drawing room with all their suffrage and nonsense about women's rights, but Camille spoke up in that hard voice I'd heard down with the Knights of Labor.

"Sit down." I wondered for a second if she had actually poisoned the old Mayor so fiercely did she speak. "The marriage is being annulled because it was never consummated." I sat down.

"Never?"

"Not even one time. You were the only man who visited my bed in 1875." There was dead silence. I looked in my glass for more bourbon, but it was empty. "Then…" She said nothing for a while as my dull Irish brain began to see the truth she was unveiling. "Jack is not – ?"

"He is."

"Why didn't you tell me? I deserved to know." The news was too much, and I felt several different sorts of tears sting my eyes. I was angry and yet stupidly happy at the same time. A damned son! My son.

"If you remember, you were set to marry Adeline Crain, who was also carrying your child, you three-balled tomcat." Clara has a harlot's mouth on her, to be sure. "I went to New York and made an arrangement with an old friend to keep little Jack from being known to the world as a bastard. I did that for him and you as well." She drained her glass and looked at me with something approaching pity. Camille spoke with a softer tone as I suppose she could see the sadness on my face.

"Now she will be free to marry you, and the boy will have a father- his father."

"And we both get you." Clara said this with her back to me as she refilled my little glass with bourbon.

"Both?" I didn't know what more to say, but they had no trouble going on explaining themselves as disciples of Mary Wollstonecraft and someone named Lucy Stone, who has similarly dangerous ideas about marriage and life in general. Neither of them are in any way fond of the state of Holy Matrimony as it limits their right to love as they wish, when they wish, with whomever they wish. The idea of some husband (they spoke the word like a curse) ruling over them made their blood boil. For my part, I was feeling some tenderness for little Jack, the poor fatherless Irish boy. I thought about the times I had seen him, how well we'd gotten along, how he had the glint of the Irish in his blue eyes. Those thoughts stilled my anger as it occurred to me that I had to strike some sort of deal with these strong women other than taking off my belt and thrashing them as my own father would have done. Clara was a rich woman who could take young Jack to New York or Cincinnati or Borneo if she chose to, and I'd never see him again.

"I think your ideas may have some flaws in them or at least many people will see them as wrong. St. Louis is not yet Paris." Camille responded immediately.

"It is the thinking of men that is flawed. They just want to control women, like slaves, and they have so precariously balanced their whole civilization on such control that they are afraid that any change will make it all come crashing down." She gave me what I think of as her Icarian look, kind, but superior to fools who don't grasp her point.

"It's hard to go against the way things have always been, even if it's right. I see that every day in politics." I was trying to give them the benefit of my experience, but they weren't having it. Clara came close now.

"It doesn't have to be the way it's always been. Not in America." They both enclosed me in a kind of an embrace that made me feel both warm and cold at the same time. Warm, because they seemed to be offering themselves, but cold in that it seemed like some kind of witches' rite that was working some magic on me. Maybe it did because I don't remember those few minutes very well. We did eventually have some supper provided by the servants who must have been hiding in the kitchen. I wanted desperately to see Jack, but his mother has strict rules about early bedtime for the boy. (That will be changing.) There was much talk on the part of both women and mostly dumbfounded listening from me.

"There are some things we will expect from you, Fergal, in this union." I gave Clara a saucy look that made both of them smile. "I need you to support the cause of women's suffrage. There will be a convention here in Saint Louis next year, and your voice could sway some of the other men in the city and gain their support."

"I don't have as much pull as you might think." They both continued to smile at me, none too sweetly. "Still, I do have Claymore's ear and he has the Mayor's."

"You are an important man, Fergal." Clara looked to Camille.

"And I want help with a much longer road, and you will have to help me with the cause of Labor surreptitiously, of course." I wrinkled my nose at the big word. "With no one knowing," she said.

I nodded. "Yes, the Unions are none too popular in these parts."

"Inch by inch, Fergal. Inch by inch. We'll change the world by a mile before you know it. Once women have the vote, they will abolish all of the laws that yoke us to the past, and we can all enjoy the blessings of Liberty." Camille took my left hand while Clara latched on to my right. We sat like that a while in silence as I grew warmer and warmer, and I found myself agreeing to the whole ridiculous plan.

I came back here now to write this, and looking over what I wrote, it shocks me in so many ways. Once men allow these women to have their own minds about how to live, the whole world will go to Hell in a handbasket. Still, I don't think either of them truly understands how the world works, that once we are married, I will be making all the decisions for wicked Clara and Camille as well. I saw a play a few years ago when the great London Shakespeare Company came to Saint Louis as all great things do. I don't remember the name of it, but it had "Shrew" in the title. In the end, the woman placed her hand beneath her husband's boot to do as he wished, and the audience, men and women, gave the actors a standing ovation. That's the true way of the world.

I imagine there will be some problems with this plan, but there's no need to fear the wind if your haystacks are tied down. Mark my words, these women will come to see me as their lord and master soon enough with the power to decide what's what. More important that any of this, I have a son, a son who will very shortly know that his father is the wildest Irishman of them all, Fergal Dunne, the Mayor's man and the damned Veiled Prophet to boot!

Chapter 34

ABIGAIL

Of course, my story did not end on the night Madame saved my life. I am still a young woman with hours and hours of life before her. There is yet a chance that my brain malady will worsen, and I will need to be shut away (even Madame cannot save me if I become a lunatic). There is also a chance that my touch of African blood will make me a pariah in society for the rest my life. Father says that Americans will soon cease to care about such things, but I am not so sure he is right. While all that may be true, I am happy enough for now. Even though it may seem foolish, I have embraced Madame's words from the night of my ordeal. I hold tightly to each moment of love when it happens, keeping it in my heart as a charm to ward off whatever suffering the world holds for me. That is the secret to being the happiest girl in Hell, in case you missed it. I also try to allow the good things that happen for others to give me joy.

For example, it seems that my father and Clara are to marry one another. I am unsure how that is possible, but I was told that soon we will live in her big house, that she will be my stepmother, and that I can have a dog. Madame Colet will also continue to tutor me and be my loving friend.

Speaking of love, I have news of dear Max. Clara (I suppose I shall be calling her "mother" soon) spoke with him only a few nights ago, pulling him away from his family at the Debar's Theatre where Mr. Edwin Booth was about to portray Hamlet. She said that Max was very nervous and upset when she brought up my name. To the good, he claimed to still feel great affection for me, but to the bad, he finds the situation with his family impossible. He said it would be difficult enough to marry a girl who was not of some German ancestry. Now that his aunt knows about the taint in my blood, anything other than a clandestine love between us would be impossible.

"Such love is stronger than family, *mon cher.*" Madame said this when Clara gave her report to us. "Look at Romeo and Juliet."

I did not point out that things did not end well for those particular star-crossed lovers who disobeyed their families. Still, maybe she is right. If Max and I have only some more small moments of happiness before the world does what it will with us, that might just be enough happiness to have. I might even remain the happiest girl in Hell for a good while yet.

By the way, I did finally read *Lalla Rookh*, the very long, popular poem by Mr. Moore. It surprised me that the Veiled Prophet in the story is a terrible villain, who seeks to destroy mankind and enslaves the poor Zelica in his harem. It would have made more sense to have a parade and ball dedicated to someone who believed in love a little bit. Of course, that is just what a mad girl thinks.

AFTERWORD

According to public records, Fergal Dunne and Clara McPherson married in 1879 in a civil ceremony. Clara stayed active in the women's suffrage movement hosting several large rallies in Saint Louis during the 1880's to include a visit from Elizabeth Cady Stanton. It seems that she had something of a war of words with Joseph Pulitzer after she wrote a letter to the *Post-Dispatch* encouraging wives to deny husbands their "conjugal rights" until they consented to support women's rights as citizens of the United States. Although the letter went unpublished in the paper, it was leaked to the public and resulted in a Post editorial that referred to Clara as a "dangerous woman who would have her sex forgo their privilege of entering lifeboats ahead of men."

It is perhaps not a coincidence that in 1883 the Dunnes sold their home in Vandeventer Place and moved to a place in Saint Louis County very near the newly constructed courthouse. Fergal became an employee of the Commissioner of Roads and one of the few prominent men named as supporting women's suffrage.

Abigail Dunne married Max Niedringhaus in 1880 at Trinity Lutheran Church in Soulard. They lived in what would become

Maplewood for a few years before moving to California. I found this letter from her to Fergal and Clara stuck in the back of his diary.

Dear Mother and Father,

I pray that this letter finds you in good health. I wanted to write sooner, but there has been much to do with all that is required of me in setting up house here in San Francisco. Our new home is small, yet quite beautiful and very near the new Golden Gate Park which is almost as grand as Forest Park. Max is excited about his position with the Belt Railroad, and the company must be happy with him as they appear to never want to let him come home. Speaking of trains, little Max is still quite delighted with the fine wooden train set that his grandparents gave him as a departing gift; he plays with it every day.

I know I spoke my heart to you both in the days before we left, but it is easier for me to write some things than say them. I love you both more than you can imagine. As a girl, I was a twisted thing destined only for the madhouse or a worse house. You stood with me to prevent that from happening. My great sorrow in leaving Saint Louis is that it will be some years before I can return and be your loving daughter again. I can only pray to God that I will be able to do that.

Please write to me as often as you can. I will need to feel your love fly from the page into my heart. I have included a letter for Madame Colet. I hope that she has fully recovered.

Your daughter,
Abigail

I did not find that letter to Madame Colet among the papers I had. There was also no mention of her in any of the public records I searched. She seems to have slipped through life unnoticed by History as most of us do, our most valuable accomplishments warranting no remarks. Still, it is possible that my hoarding family will unearth more material (they have all vowed to search). We shall wait and see.